Sophia Lorena Benjamin

CLAUDIA

NIYOGI BOOKS

Published by
NIYOGI BOOKS
Block D, Building No. 77,
Okhla Industrial Area, Phase-I,
New Delhi-110 020, INDIA
Tel: 91-11-26816301, 26818960
Email: niyogibooks@gmail.com
Website: www.niyogibooksindia.com

Editor: Gita Rajan
Design: Nabanita Das

ISBN: 978-93-86906-29-8
Publication: 2018

Printed at: Niyogi Offset Pvt. Ltd., New Delhi, India

My Husband, Clement Benjamin,
who helped me to reach out to things
I thought impossible.

Hay bed and mist

3:20 am

In a little while, the dark clouds would part the hillock, night dew losing its vigour to daylight. Cradling glory in its chest like a singer ready to burst into song, with a readiness to inspire a new day, a new life, was the sun; still to rise on the first day of October 1961 when Claudia changed her cotton house dress; white and blue polka dots over a faded orange background, curry-stained pockets on either side of its skirt. She grabbed a piece of coal, leftover from the night's cooking fire to clean her teeth. She gargled, hurriedly, ran wet fingers through her long, black hair, and lo! She was ready to meet her man. Her crime, her love, her Damiáno.

She should have been at the ruins by that time, but for the dream. The dream delayed her; she woke up, groaning, moaning, almost agonising and letting out soft sobs as the dream caused her mind and body to convulse in quick bursts of uncontrolled release.

Damiáno was strongly present in the dream, but still the dream seemed bad, well; part good, part bad. She clearly remembered he was running. Chased by black butterflies, like fairies with pitch black feathers, surrounding him from all sides.

In the dream, Claudia desperately tried to follow him, to try and help, but he sped, running faster than her, disappearing into an obscure remoteness.

The previous day, the fish market reeked of rumours, about the Portuguese leaving.

'Goa may become a part of India' was the hush-hush talk.

Aroused with curiosity, Claudia mustered courage to linger close to the men in the tanno, the local market, as close as she possibly could. She casually walked through the damp lanes of the market, as each breath of her nostrils filled with the strong smell of fresh sea fish. She carefully drowned all other sounds to grasp every word of gossip uttered by ageing village elders. A sudden smile escaped her lips when she realised how close she had got to the village elders, without their knowing that she was listening in to their banter. She felt proud of her boldness.

The boldness gave way to a feeling of abject fear when the realisation of what she just heard became clear.

'The Portuguese cannot go!' A voice screamed from deep within, and tears engulfed her eyes with intense speed, like waves swelling up and swirling towards the dry shore.

The Portuguese presence in Goa evoked much reaction from the local population who recorded conversations about them in various shades and slants. There was so much talk that went around surrounding their every action. One such instance that gained significance was about how the Portuguese Admiral Afonso de Albuquerque took possession of Goa from Yusuf Adil Shah, the Muslim ruler who controlled the Sultanate of Bijapur. Ever since the takeover, the Portuguese had become an integral part of Goa and the Goan population, for more than 400 years. The Portuguese had won the hearts of the masses. Many folks, the Catholics in particular, had begun to highly regard the Portuguese, at least that's what everyone in Oroshim was talking about.

The talk at the local bazaars, the taverns, the balcao meetings, very often dominated the Portuguese and their wondrous works as to how they influenced the villas in Goa—bright coloured walls with white painted bordering, the open air balcaos with inbuilt seating, where folks took pleasure in sitting especially for an evening chat with their neighbours. They spoke about how the Portuguese made Goa the largest territory of Portuguese India and a main centre for spice trading in the region. They discussed how the Portuguese imported milk, milk powder, cheese and biscuits from Portugal which was distributed among the lesser privileged, especially young children and babies whose parents couldn't afford milk.

They said it was the Portuguese who influenced and educated the Goan folk on European manners, style of dressing as well as taking great pride in wearing fabrics of high quality and living merrily.

One domineering aspect of the Portuguese was that they were keen observers of formalities and a people who respected authority. They assigned much importance to appearance with special emphasis on dining and social etiquette, they even taught the Goan people to greet each other with a tight handshake and a warm hug.

It was the Portuguese who ushered in the influence of these elements into the cultural fabric of Goa. The ballroom dancing, elegant parties with live music and singing, joyful wedding celebrations, the mando—the romantic expression through song and dance. It was all a confluence of the best of Portuguese culture and traditions that merged with the local atmosphere.

With such deep impact on the societal, cultural and lifestyle aspects, it was only a matter of time for the influence to permeate Goan cuisine. Portuguese forms of eating, cooking, and recipes soon became an integral part of the local food. It was apparent through the rich and exotic Bebinca with its thick layered base of egg batter, the spicy and sumptuous Chouricos, Galinha Cafreal, Assada, Caldeirada, Racheido and Feijoada. All of which, Portuguese in influence.

Subsequently, for generations, the stories of how despite opposition and attacks from Adil Shah and probably even the Marathas, Goa went on to become the centre of Portuguese India continued to dominate every household. Even after India achieved Independence, France, who then occupied Pondicherry, handed it back to India; but the Portuguese held on to Goa, in spite of the Nehru government's insistence. This gave rise to the entry of the *satyagrahis* from Independent India, who dared to come to Goa and challenge the Portuguese.

This caused Claudia to think, what then happened to Goa Dourada, the Golden Goa that the educated folks of Goa celebrated in their conversations? What happened to the Goa that was spoken of to have reached the peak of its success and had gathered vast profits through shipment of spices to Europe and grown in popularity for its marvellous architectural beauty, she wondered.

It was popularly known that the Portuguese had literally left no stone unturned in developing Goa to resemble Lisbon; the architecture, the streets, the charming cobbled pavements, the railings, and more. They built houses that were uniquely Portuguese—beautiful arches and winding staircases, they built the baroque style Churches, they built chapels, the bazaars and more and it all suited their taste and style. It had apparently seemed that the Portuguese were here to stay.

And with all the development they did to make Goa look like Lisbon, shouldn't the Portuguese feel at home? Then, why should they leave? Claudia argued in her mind. The thoughts grieved her.

Claudia's beautiful dark eyes welled up as she recollected the gossip at the fish market and then the troubling dream she just had about Damiáno. She was wide awake now, staring into the hollow pre-dawn darkness, lying restlessly on the bamboo mat; its protruding parts poking her back. In the darkness outside, she could hear the owls hoot.

The peaceful coolness of the early morning caressed her to sleep again but it wasn't a long one. It felt like she woke up almost as quickly as she fell asleep as she realised Damiáno was still in the village, and not running away as in her dream.

With sudden urgency she realised that they were supposed to meet in a few moments.

She adored those meetings with him, although the village had its own rules; stinging, unsparing rules that made her feel that her time with her Portuguese lover was no more than lustful contact. Maybe it was.

She was just a simple girl from the local village, working as a maid in his house.

All that she had to do was to draw water from the well, sweep the floors of the spacious mansion, tidy up the beds, wash clothes and do other chores as required. That was her job. That was what she was paid for. He was Portuguese, the master class. There was no way she could expect someone like him to marry her. The servant class.

Father slept on his cot, snoring loudly. Jakin snored as well and Mother was in deep slumber. Bula muttered senselessly in her sleep. To Claudia, she didn't make much sense when awake either. The moment Claudia sat up, Bula grabbed her pillow; made up of used clothes, but soft and comfortable enough to give rest to a tired head. Pillow snatching was common among the family of five with three pillows. Mostly it was Jakin, Bula and Claudia who took turns to share one pillow among them, as with their clothes, especially any new dress, bickering over who would get to wear it first. Being the eldest, Jakin would always get away with wearing any new dress; unless it was something that didn't fit or something she didn't fancy much.

Blankets, however, did not pose a problem. The house had plenty of jute sacks, the ones that Paklin Bai disposed off after buying her monthly stock of coconuts and grocery. The jute sacks were really good, and when dusted, cut open and piled up one on top of the other, turned into warm, soft blankets for use to sleep on or cover during winter.

It is the onset of the winter of 1961; The Goan beaches are tranquil and unspoilt. Most houses are made of natural resources; walls with mud and laterite, roofs with weaved palms and coconut trunk beams. Their diet is mostly rice and fish, prepared with whole spices and coconut, pounded over a granite stone, sometimes for as long as an hour to get the desired consistency. Their local drink is made out of fresh palm toddy and cashew fruits. They grow fruits and vegetables in their backyard and breed chickens and pigs; much of it for their personal consumption.

Their surroundings are full of trees and bushes, their doors wide open to enjoy the natural breeze. Dances and weddings are celebrated in wide open spaces fenced with trees and palms.

Unlike neighbouring Bombay, there are no Beachside Hotels and Resorts in Goa. If the fishermen or the toddy tappers are not at work, the seaside is mostly lonely with no inhabitants around. The fisher folks are commonly seen at dawn each day. After casting their nets at night, they return in the morning to the sea to drag in the nets with the catch of fish. Soon after sunrise, they separate the different kinds of fish. Some of the catch is transported to the local market and some is spread out for drying after coating with a lavish application of salt; a natural preservative. Thereafter, the fishing nets are washed, cleaned and spread out for drying.

As for the toddy tapper, he is seen acrobatically climbing the palm trees with a sharp sickle and a pot hung across his waist to gather the sap from the palm tree. He cheerfully sings loud songs in his own rhythm and melody with a musical whistle that reverberates across the landscaped meadows. Popularly called as *rendher mama,* or toddy tapper uncle, he deftly climbs down the tall, lanky palm tree with his pot full of toddy which is then fermented to turn into an intoxicating palm feni, an ethereal local drink.

Goa and its villages are sprawled across hills and valleys, lush green fields and sparkling, meandering rivulets. The traditional paddy fields and luscious hilltops add intrigue to the beauty and solitude. The large patches of thick bushes and dense trees make the surroundings open and airy, also providing intriguing places of secrecy and privacy with no disturbance for miles around.

The winter nights are chilled, with cold winds blowing across the fields. With no electricity, the nights, unless it is a full moon, are pitch dark. The Oroshim villagers always work a way around their circumstances, at night they carry a thick, long torch: dried palm leaves lit up with fire. Most homes have adopted a watch dog, not entertained to come inside the house; it eats, sleeps and guards the house from outside. The stillness of the night is disturbed only when the dogs alert the villagers each time someone passes by too close to their house. The only sounds that can be heard apart from the intermittent barking of dogs is an occasional mooing of cows, the flapping of night birds, owls hooting in the distance and the sounds of the male crickets calling out to attract the female and repel other males; a sound which is piercingly loud and overpowers all other sounds.

Claudia drew the coarse jute covering close to her chest. It was pitch dark, and cold.

She contemplated the dream again. Father's watch lay on the kitchen table. It was an old watch, pieces of tiny thread stuck out of its worn out leather strap but it helped keeping track of time. An even more worn out leather wallet; filled with bills that Father owed liquor bar owners rested next to the watch.

Through the heavy blackness, Claudia soundlessly made her way to the table. Softly dropping the watch in the pocket of her cotton dress, she headed towards the kitchen. Not that she was ignorant of the possibility of Father waking up, she was, her mind alert and conscious not to forget the terrible consequences of the sin of stepping out to meet a man in the dark.

She knew there was a possibility of being caught, exposed, if Father came to know.

Just one drunken evening from him was enough to ruin her reputation forever.

Yet the attraction that Damiáno drew her with was much too strong and exciting for her to deny herself the opportunity to spend time with him. No matter what the cost. The matchbox took eight strikes to light up the matchstick. The dried palm leaves flared up easily once they caught the flame. The watch dial was now clearly visible in the light of the flame.

3:25 am

If she didn't hasten, it would be dawn in another hour and thirty five minutes. Despite the hurry, something took her back to the dream. The villagers always had interpretations for dreams. A dream about death meant something good was going to happen. Something bad was on, if it was a wedding. A priest meant something sad was about to take place. Seeing lost loved ones meant protection. But seeing a lover rûn in a dream? She had never heard of a dream like that before. And she struggled to comprehend it.

The elderly learned in the village spoke of a dream as an intuitive caution; some said they were ready-to-occur events secretly sharing a preview of things to come. This time, Claudia was not inclined to place her faith in the village elders' beliefs. As she made her way cautiously to the ruins, the dream continued to haunt her. Buzzing bees ... black butterflies ... blowing breeze ... Damiáno...

'Late, late, late,' she whined between hurried steps which would get her to the gum tree where they always met. As she vigorously paced the last few steps, she caught a glimpse of his unmistakable silhouette leaning against the tree, calm, arms folded, right leg crossed over the left, waiting for her. In spite of the distance and the darkness, she was absolutely sure the shadow belonged to Damiáno. It was like she could just feel him deep inside herself and it wasn't just the silhouette that was needed to confirm his presence. She just knew.

The moment he saw her emerge through the darkness he shone the light of his torchlight straight into her eyes. This is something he often did. It was his way of welcoming her, teasing her. First, he let the torch light up her path towards him, and then, when she came closer, he shone it straight into her eyes, blinding her for a few moments, just to enjoy the thrill of her feeling her way towards him.

She blinked and put her hand to shield her eyes from the bright light and slowed down her steps to cover the remaining distance as she neared him, but could not slow down the rapid pounding of her excited heart. She paused, but only for a moment to catch her breath, gasping with the thrilled excitement of those last few steps, before flinging herself right into his open arms as he drew her tightly against his chest. She could almost hear her heart pounding. Today, however, her feelings were different. She was worried and excited at the same time! She contemplated telling him about the dream that troubled her. More than that, she was anxious to ask him if the talk about the Portuguese leaving India was true. With the thoughts pounding her heart and mind, she remained silent. She was not sure if she was ready to hear his response. At least not yet.

The shaky ting tong when Damiáno pressed his thumb on the campaignha, the metallic bell, of his Atlas bicycle seemed too loud in the morning stillness. Amused, Claudia smiled and shushed him with a finger on her lips, not wanting anyone to stumble on to their little secret. The bumpy drive was their first ride together. She felt silly to sit side-saddle on the bar of his bicycle, holding on to the handle as her legs swayed. Strong breeze ruffled their hair; the early morning chill almost biting every part of exposed skin. He halted the drive briefly to wrap a woollen muffler to cover his ears and then took his soft cotton handkerchief to wrap it around her head. As he pedalled again, the wind continued to blow. As the cycle moved through the mud road, a small bump opened out her loosely twisted hair and soft tangles covered her face and cheeks. Her loose hair billowing around her face brought out a raw innocent look.

A clear unblemished complexion adding to her feminine charm. Rice flour! That's what Father would call her during her younger days because of her smooth, fair skin. Now, however, her skin looked a bit wheatish against Damiáno's white Mediterranean skin.

But for the sound of breeze and the squishing of the cycle tyres on the muddy road, the village was quiet. Damiáno pedalled his way along the rough road, laced with dark red mud, carefully manoeuvred through the uneven bumps, across the narrow bunds, meandering between large spaces of thistle and hay strewn all around. The sour smell of mouldy wet hay and stale water from the dormant puddles and idle ponds filled the air.

'Would you like to ride, my dear?' he asked, with a genuine plea in his voice as though it was a gift being offered to make her happy. They had reached the soft tambdimati road. The twenty minutes ride took them out of Oroshim and into another waddo, a little village with fewer inhabitants than Claudia's village.

'Not sure I can Bab. No practice. Long time since Father sold his cycle.'

'*Muito Bem*!' He said excitedly. 'Which means you can ride.'

'*Muito Bem*, Very Well,' a common Portuguese expression, was his favourite phrase to cheer her and it always brought a smile and a blush to her face.

'I need to practise again, Bab,' she said. In Claudia's village, Bab was what you called someone you respected, so she called him Damiáno Bab.

'Why did he sell the cycle dear?' he enquired while getting off and helping Claudia straddle the cycle to ride.

'Because he had lost his job. Remember Bab, I told you they closed down the place he worked at?'

Claudia pushed on the pedal, as he sat on the back. At first the bicycle wobbled and Claudia struggled to steady it; he was a well set man and heavy. But she was a strong village girl and soon gained control and balance. The season's first berries dropping from the borom trees made a squishing noise under the front wheel of the cycle, crushing as the lovers rode away from the familiar surroundings of Oroshim. It would soon be dawn.

'*Muito Bem*! Was he working at one of those printing presses?' he asked.

'Oh Yes. You're right. How did you guess that, Bab?'

'Ah, I heard about it. The government closed down many of the printing presses.'

'The Indian Government?'

'Oh No. Not the Indians. These decisions are taken in Portuguese India.'

'But why?'

'Hmm. It's complicated Claudia. It's the way the government functions. António de Oliveira Salazar, it seems, is rigid about the way he controls law and order. However, I don't think we should talk about these issues. Slow! Slow! Slow down, dear.' he exclaimed as the cycle gained speed down a slope.

'Please tell me Bab, I want to know why my family was the only one needy, poor and deprived in all of Oroshim.'

'Look out! Steady the front wheel! Didn't I ask you to slow down, dear?' he said as he wrapped his hands around her waist.

'Poor Father. How could they do that to him? You didn't answer my question Bab.'

'What question?'

'Why are they closing down the printing presses?'

'*Minha querida*, I said no speed. Turn this way. Don't take the river lane. Too cold there. Turn around.'

'This way?' She questioned on taking a right at the crossroads.

'Yes. *Muito Bem.* So what was your question?'

'Baaaab,' she whimpered.

'What is it, my dear?'

'Why are they closing down the printing press?'

'The printing press. Hmm, how do I explain?'

'Bab just....'

'Alright alright, have you heard of the Colonial Act? There are restrictions placed on liberties, under special law, on the press. As in, when it comes to censorship. Uh ... how do I explain it all to you Claudia? Let's say media resources like books and other printed material have to be submitted for approval from the Governor before publication.'

'And then ...?' Claudia questioned, trying to conceal her inability to understand the context of the politics involved; as a self-schooled girl, drawing all her knowledge from the houses she worked at, politics and intricate government affairs made little sense to her.

'Difficult to comprehend, isn't it? *Minha querida*, we don't have to discuss this.'

'Please.'

'Alright. Let me try. You see all publishing houses are prohibited from circulating any printed material without censorship. Also no public meetings of political nature can be conducted without prior approval from the authorities. So yes, any printing press that fails to adhere to such prerequisites will in all likelihood be shut down.'

He explained patiently, and as he spoke, his grip on her waist tightened.

'You are tickling me, Bab.' she giggled, ignoring the staggering bicycle and its swaying wheels, blushing with joy as she continued to pedal.

The toughness of her working hands, as she gripped the handlebar, the soft rise and fall of her arms as they exposed her tender armpits through the loose sleeves of her pink and white chiffon dress, her smile, the feminine delicateness of her narrow waist; all of it brought out an ethereal charm that was hard to ignore.

Claudia was a desirable young woman who possessed naive warmth but harboured sharp instincts, to an extent that made her appear clever, almost. She was endowed with an alert shrewdness imbibed from a harsh and tough upbringing. Overall, what Claudia displayed was raw, natural and refreshing beauty that could attract any man.

'Should I take my hands off then?' Damiáno muttered with a naughty tone in his voice.

'No. Hold me. I like it.'

'Ok. But only if you stop babbling and asking heavy questions, it doesn't suit a pretty face like yours.'

'Stop here, *minha querida.*' Damiáno instructed, and she braked carefully.

She absolutely loved it each time he called her *minha querida*, that cherished Portuguese term for 'my dear.' Once the bicycle was parked on its stand, she led him to the top of the haystack. She climbed the tall pile of hay first, almost like it was something all too easy and then held out her hand to pull him up. She felt like a passionate princess enticing her first love onto a secret tower. He hesitated for a moment but decided to give in, amused at her adventurous mischief. He took off the woollen *kambou* wrapped around him and spread it across the damp hay; and she took off her white cotton *ole* to use it to cover them both as they lay side by side on their back on the top of the haystack. It wasn't easy to come this far out of Oroshim. Such an act called for a different sort of boldness; and this is what they had braved very often, ever since the first time it had started and had now increased in frequency. These meetings had since increased in urgency as they both braved the twilight darkness of many new moon nights, stealing away from the village, the people, their family and choosing the thrill of spending forbidden time together in the cold winter mornings.

The air was cold as it swept across the fields. They lay cradled in each other's arms on the dew-damp hay. Deep, long-drawn kisses and the warmth of their aroused bodies was the only thing keeping them warm. His strong palms bore her down on the hay, as he rose to come on top of her. He was always the first one to make a move, the first one in choosing his own liberties with her. And she didn't object. Neither the falling dew, nor the overbearing smell of damp hay bothered that moment.

Everything felt vague and still in those dark moments, except their bodies; in the darkness, two shadows blended, merged as one, only to disunite for brief moments before rejoining again. No one in Oroshim knew the haystack was often occupied in a wrong manner like that. The act, if brought to light, could cost Claudia untold damage. No girl in Oroshim was supposed to enjoy that kind of freedom; especially no unmarried young girl. Still, Claudia broke all the established rules in order to spend affectionate, passionate, intimate time with her white skinned Portuguese lover.

The haystack, painstakingly built by the farmers to be used as cattle feed, to ripen fruits, to cook fresh sardines, was an integral part of the village community. One reason why kids caught climbing on top of the haystack got their bottoms spanked. The very same forbidden haystack in the dark early morning hours; gave Damiáno and Claudia unrestrained privacy to do things they could never do at most other places. Though their meetings seemed more like physical appointments meant to gratify fleshy lust, they rejoiced in it. Those moments spent with Damiáno were the only pleasurable moments of Claudia's life, for as long as she could remember.

As the darkness began to fade and the orangey gold of the sunrise began to reveal the surroundings, Claudia drew herself away with suddenness from Damiáno's arms. Any moment the rooster would crow, alerting the village to wake up to a new dawn. The bread man honking his horn; housewives stepping out, eager to meet a man who is not their father, brother or husband, yet the one they waited for each morning. Blushing at the first sight of him; revelling in the nonsensical anecdotes of his life experiences, drawing excitement and shyness at his flirtatious remarks. Those fleeting moments of flirtation with another man was enough to put a smile on their face. Claudia, on the other hand, would desperately look forward to meet Damiáno with an agonising longing that was hard to contain; each night, she would look forward to the time when the whole of Oroshim went back to sleep.

Surrounded by little hillocks, Oroshim's mornings were normal, unexceptional. Noisy chickens scratched through its fertile earth seeking worms and pecked away with their beaks after scratching the earth, the multi-coloured rooster with its proud prancing dared folks to wake up at dawn with loud and repetitive wake up calls, through continuous crowing. The local men and women relieved themselves each morning in home built lavatories carrying metallic tin containers filled with water. Most families in the village lived in conventional conditions, but almost everyone owned a mud house with a thatched-roof toilet that had access to the nearby bushes. It was not unusual for pigs visiting the toilets freely, oinking around hungrily.

Occasionally, an expectant hen would carefully choose a spot in its owner's backyard to lay eggs, cautiously glaring at everything around to ensure the safety of the egg. The hen would drop her smooth little oval wonder and come out announcing it with her protective, loud clucking. Cluck cluck cluckaaawk cluck. Was it a typical female spirit that dominated the village?

Perhaps. That's why it wasn't surprising to see the women of Oroshim display a cautious alertness when it came to their offspring, especially when it involved their daughters.

Each morning, soon after dawn, women awoke after a dull eventless night to go through their daily chores. The first task would be to wash previous night's used utensils, with a piece of coir made up from dried husk dipped in soft grey ash collected from the burnt out firewood.

When the seasons changed, the morning scene altered just a little. During peak summer, the farm folk placed oversized copper pots on fire in the open yards, much before dawn, and boiled the harvested rice grains to be dried in the scorching sun at noon. The grain would then be ready to be home-milled for a good stock of rice.

Rice was a dominant part of the village life. Daily diet included ample amounts of rice; during afternoon and night meals, morning *ambil*, evening snacks, rice kanji (for hunger and fever), roasted rice as a digestive decoction. At times, a generous offering of raw rice was a gift to a loved one, a display of kindness; even beggars who went house to house and chanted with a chain of rosary beads were offered a handful of rice in dried, empty coconut shells. Beside all this, summer mornings displayed one common scene; bare-chested men bathing by the well, rubbing thick, brownish yellow, *Cycle Chaap* washing soap over their bodies while the women stood by to draw water for their men and scrub their backs.

Four demanding months of sweltering, hot and sweaty summer heat was replaced by the torrential monsoon rains:

Oroshim readying itself to mesmerise, especially its visitors, with a captivating aura of its own, the quiet cool, sunless calm and the scenic charm of the monsoon. The wind came in broken spells and sudden bursts of thunder. The same wind bent the tall, lanky coconut trees and got them to bow down to salute the sea. Broken tree branches were everywhere along with mangoes, dried palms and coconuts mixed with broken parts of thatched huts. Wild flowers bloomed in glorious colours and green grass turned greener, the colour of life springing up everywhere. Buds began to flower on the trees, adding a splash of colour. The taller stalks of grass swayed with a *mando* like rhythm, nodding their heads in delight. At times the sun cautiously peeped through the clouds. White mogras spread a perfumed, sweet flowery scent. Oroshim experienced many days of inescapable wetness, resembling a rain-stunned garden; lush and bountiful. After a brief interval, chaotic raindrops densely dropped over ponds and rivers in splashes, spreading ripples with each fall, quickly taking the shape of wild slushy streams within streams rushing to meet the sea. The rain filled up the wells and raised it to a level that could be drawn even with a child's bare hand.

Long ferry boats wobbled with every wave as the rough monsoon wind blew across the deep sea. Incessantly strong winds, sudden thunderstorms and the high waves forced the fishermen to anchor their fishing boats high up the sea face, away from the waves; the power of those waves and winds retold with real experiences by many a fisherman who warned the adventurous novices from venturing out to sea. The classic smell of fish was unusually absent in the otherwise busy fish market.

Houses that filled the nostrils of passersby with the smell of typical Goan fish curry now released a different odour of a Goan curry prepared with onion, tomato and *sol*, (dried skin of a unique fruit found on the local hills) substituted for fish. Salt fish now appeared prominent and the strong, salty smell permeated the atmosphere at mealtimes. Pickled whole green mangoes; stored when raw, in thick white marble jars with brown lids were sliced as an accompaniment to the rice and curry.

Most of the deep, low lying areas, filled with the brown slushy water took days to dry, making it difficult to commute. The vast expanses of rice fields were clothed in a brilliant green covering and indigenously designed raincoats made with palm leaves appeared on bunds and fields as the villagers tried their best to shield themselves from the blowing wind and incessant rain. Quaint liquor bars, located at short distances from each other all around the tambdimati lanes and by-lanes displayed curious sounding Portuguese names; Casa de Antok, Caravela, Rosa Tavern, Sol e Pesca; they readied themselves to serve their thirsty patrons. The bars provided a welcome abode for the rain drenched, hardworking, cold and wet men to huddle together and indulge in moments of unhindered, simple luxury. At every opportunity, Oroshim did not disappoint those seeking rustic beauty, mingled uniquely with the laid-back lifestyle and simplistic living.

Many years back, before their three daughters Jakin, Bula and Claudia were born, Claudia's parents had spent a couple of laborious days and nights building their house with mud. The house was hand-built, with friends and neighbours joining in using earth from the land, a few raw bricks, wood from fallen trees and bamboo. A little cement was used to hold together windows and a door. This way of construction was what was learnt by observing their fathers and grandfathers build houses when they were children. They enjoyed watching them build it and remembered the techniques used where mud was mixed with water and left to become sticky. The roof was made from woven coconut fronds with a framework of bamboo and coconut trunk beams, cut skilfully before the hand crafted country tiles were placed over the framework. The flooring was coated with cow dung and outer walls with lime for waterproofing and repelling insects.

What joy it was for Claudia's parents and the neighbourhood to stand back and admire the completion of a secure shelter for another of their beloved village folk to live in. Claudia's father had hosted a little celebration immediately after the successful construction of *mattiechem ghor*, the hand-built mud house, with a bottle of cashew feni and chicken xacuti.

Once upon a time, Claudia's family was all that a family should be; happy, content and united. Then life's journey brought them to face unexpected challenges. Bad luck is what they blamed it on, but they had also made a few naive choices. Adventurous urges, bold desires and blinding temptations led them away from the safety of the harsh village rules and boundaries to a wrongly perceived sense of freedom. They were fortunate not to be thrown out of their home and village for some of the acts committed. In spite of the many mistakes; they were still a part of Oroshim, their beautiful village.

Much of Oroshim's natural beauty came from an extension of a river; the locals called it 'Zorii.' The river water sparkled in the sun, as the tall grass swayed in the soft breeze. Palm trees stood tall and proud on the other side of the river, and beyond the fields to the rear of the river rose great hills as well as little hillocks.

The calm river flowed with clear water and threw reflections on the steeple above the cream-white church extending into a tall cross. Winding pathways and rich hues of red mud laced the suburban lanes where bougainvillea and hibiscus flowers bloomed wild. Cashew trees, paddy fields with bunds, tall coconut palms and lush green shrubs dotted the village. The long stretch of beach, below the hillside, was mostly occupied by fisher folks busy with their usual fishing activities, except during monsoon.

Damiáno and Claudia chose to stay away from the romantic beauty of the village, preferring to meet outside of Oroshim much before dawn broke out; the dark early morning hour was the only time of the day that could be safe for their privacy. Damiáno's cycle lay parked near the haystack, by Tukaram's milk farm, where cows and oxen and buffaloes woke up under a thatched roof. It wouldn't be long when Tukaram would be out of his hut to begin milking his cows and buffaloes. Damiáno rode speedily; ensuring Claudia made it back to her house before the sun could come out, and escape being seen; a young, local servant girl from the village and her rich and suave Portuguese master; a sight that could amount to blasphemy in Oroshim, if caught. Lucky, as an occasional fish escaping the fisherman's net leaping back into the vast sea, gliding away with brisk motions of its tailfin, was Claudia.

For a while now, she had been waking early, meeting her lover secretly, risking the walk through the village lanes alone in pitch dark, doing the forbidden; things she thought she'd be doing only with a husband. Things not supposed to be done before marriage and certainly not with a Portuguese man like Damiáno. How and when did it all start? Her thoughts took her back to the time it all happened, the monsoon.

The Sao Joao Sagor jump

24 June, 1961

Sao Joao festival! A day of fun, a day when men in Oroshim, and all over Goa, gather around wells; singing, diving and frolicking, through the first pouring rains. Rain water, self-harvested in the provincial wells, that rise at least seven times higher than the normal water levels. The men, the ones who dare, love to have a few good dives in those swelling waters. 'Sao Joao Sagor!' the village men sang, making a stop at every suburban well. As per custom, a newly married man accompanied the festival participants. This fellow found an opportunity to bask in the attention, as everyone fussed around him, the highlight of the event being the crowning of the newlywed with a crown, made up of dry thorns, flowers or even fruits. Throughout all the frenzied activity, village folk enjoyed the liquor and platters of fruits sent by the newlywed man's in-laws, as was customary. The significance of marriage in most parts of Portuguese colonised Goa was high. That and the festivals. The Sao Joao festival in particular was linked with newlyweds.

Claudia watched the merry makers from behind the partially closed window of her house, harbouring resentment within. It had been many years since her family had continually longed for a wedding in the house, in vain!

Shouts of Sao Joao Sagor were now nearing Claudia's water well. Though her two older sisters got out to join the fun, Claudia chose to remain inside. Most men would be well drunk before they were done visiting all of the shortlisted water wells in the locality. Loud and absurd arguments would follow. Men would group together and divide themselves against one another. Friends for years suddenly opposing one another only to realise their wrong, not much later, the same men got pally again, to fight with another man within the group, and the frenzied nonsense would continue.

Claudia watched silently as the men sang local Goan songs in a loud voice; singing and revelry may have been a nuisance to sober spectators, but Claudia found it to be much better in comparison to what her father did. While most men got high on spirits; drinking in celebration of Sao Joao; her father seemed to drink only to beat depression, that's why those men seemed like winners. To Claudia, everyone and everything had begun to look like winners compared to her family. The Sao Joao festival too did not grab her interest, like it did, once, years ago.

She remembered the times when Father celebrated the festival. He suddenly seemed to come alive during that time. He would bring large portions of pork sausages and take it to his friend Caitu, the baker. Together they would prepare stuffed sausage rolls in the furnace. 'Was the sausage lady so attractive?' Mother would taunt in jealousy on seeing the large amount of sausages he brought home. Instead of getting irritated, Mother's nagging would make Father laugh and ignore the comment altogether. He would throw his arms around her; strong arms that once made Mother feel safe. Father, well respected by the village folks in those days, would serve his friends well; good food to eat and good cashew feni to drink. Not many could compete with him in the traditional Sao Joao competition of fetching the cashew feni bottle pitched right at the bottom of the water well. With his raw natural energy and stamina he used to be a great swimmer and could hold his breath longer under water than most other people, without struggling.

Claudia continued to watch, as she stood behind the partially shut window of her mud house; one more group of men approached the water well, a special group it appeared, with village elders like Luis Bakaar, Botelho Bab, Simoes Bab and many more; each influential and rich in his own way. They were happy men; with time, money and reason to party. The best wine, the best food and money. They had it all. They were the elite of the village, always well dressed in well-cut suits and expensive ties, smoking fine cigars and sipping rich beer. These were in a comfortable position to settle their daughters as soon as they reached a marriageable age with an influential, rich and eligible bachelor of their choice, one reason perhaps, their daughters neither shamed their families nor were desperate to seek male attention like Bula, Jakin and Claudia.

As she continued to watch and feel the hurt of watching the rich folk revel in the festival, she suddenly observed Oliveira Bab, Paklin Bai's husband, coming onto the scene. Talking of Paklin Bai, she was a kind of mistress that anybody in Claudia's village would dream to work for; her kind-heartedness that made one spend more time with her, her cheerful nature and her love for wine that made her look charmingly funny, her generosity, her smile, and above all her talkativeness that revealed so much about her family members.

With a quick short jerk Claudia drew the curtain to hide her face. As a servant in Paklin Bai's house she had been instructed and had come to hold high esteem for Oliveira Bab. She couldn't let him look at her watching. Botelho Bab: a gold, ivory and agricultural trader and one of the village elders was there too. It was the appearance of an unfamiliar, different and new person in the assembly that got her attention. One look at him made her heart begin to race. Something about his tall figure and his masculinity.

Could this be Damiáno Bab? She had heard Paklin Bai talk much about her son who was supposed to arrive in Goa. Common folk in the village were expected to treat the village elders with respect, that's why, Claudia stretched her head out, 'Need something, Ti Botelho?' she asked. 'Claudia! You are here? Bring the drawing pot, child.' Botelho demanded in his usual commanding style.

She quickly found the pot, happy to get another chance to take a good look at the young stranger. 'Draw some water girl, and pour on Bab Damiáno's feet. They got stuck in rain slush. He's just come to Oroshim today and I am taking him around to show him how beautiful our village is. We should not give our young visitor a reason to be disappointed with our village, should we, Claudia?' Bothelho's middle-aged laughter rang across the well.

The young man looked into her eyes when she poured the water on his feet and smiled at her, expressing thanks, with a boyish grin. He was tall and his broad shoulders gave him a muscular appearance. He walked with confidence and his big hands swayed gracefully with his gait. He had wavy hair, brownish with a few gold streaks. What made him stand out were his smoothly rounded cheekbones over a V shaped face. He spoke with kindness and exuded a robust charm with an infectious, generous smile that lit up his stubble face and reflected in his warm, clear turquoise eyes. She was drawn to his crimson toned fair face; must have been wine or the afternoon sun, that flushed his face red, whatever it was, he had a colour of skin that most women in Oroshim would go mad after. Claudia instantly liked him.

Her guess was right after all. It was Damiáno Bab! The name so fondly uttered by Paklin Bai. If Botelho had asked her to take the white Bab around the village, she would have done it gladly, Claudia thought to herself. She liked helping a lot. She had the experience of assisting old Gormai get through the hilly paths; she had also helped Karmin Timai in walking to the goldsmith's remote house and had often picked up milk for Paklin Bai all the way from milkman Tukaram's house. And when someone in the village fell ill, it was Claudia who was called to rush all the way to bring Doctor Kasim, through shortcuts that not many knew of. She knew the way through the beach lanes better than most others, as well as the easy routes through the tambdimati lanes. She was the one who found neem leaves, when someone needed them to cure a skin infection, datura leaves too. Black plums for kidney stone cure. Cactus fruits for a stubborn cough. Betel nuts for reapers to chew on and berry leaves for her grandmother's cigar. Claudia knew a lot about the places to go to in the village.

The water from the leaking roof continued to drip drop by drop into the big, copper pot, old, damaged and tarnished in patches. Cold breeze swept across the meadow; it was one of those mornings, when, even the rooster and the chirpy morning birds lay down lazily. But not Claudia. She possessed a different kind of energy. Blame it on the overnight rains; for a silent morning. Except for the occasional dripping of raindrops into the copper pot, it was quiet.

Claudia regretted forcing her sisters to wake up early, shaking her head in disgust to see how silly they behaved. Their silly laughter, their cheap gossip; all of it sounding nonsensical. Not that the girls were not wise enough to realise it would get them nowhere; they knew it alright. But the choices at their disposal to keep themselves engaged in, to attempt getting some male attention, was limited. And that's why they gave in to silly behaviour.

'He is coming back, coming back!' Bula announced, jumping up and down excitedly. 'Who is coming back?' Jakin asked, her eyes glowing at the mention of a man. 'Senhor Damiáno. I thought he'd take another route to go back, but no. Hurra!' Bula overreacted.

'Sshh!' Claudia tried to silence them. They ignored her. 'Sshh!' Claudia hissed again. They paid no heed. Jakin's laughter was an act; you could tell she did not enjoy that ragging.

'And how is throwing a rotten mango at someone, hurra?' Claudia asked, annoyed at Bula. In reality what Claudia hated was the thought of her sisters getting attention from Damiáno. She had begun to secretly like him ever since the first time she had seen him and had poured well water on his feet.

'He saw me with all these mangoes. He was looking at me, and now he will think it's me who did it.' Claudia said, in an attempt to somehow try and stop her sisters from ragging him.

'Foolish girl, don't you know he was only staring at your thighs? You think he is interested in mangoes?' Increasingly insensitive with her words, Bula, the second born among the sisters, snapped back rudely. Life for the girls seemed to have lost its sensitivity gradually. They displayed little or no affection nor retained any politeness towards each other. It was as though love and respect in the family was dead.

With her skirt hitched up and held in place with both arms at her waist, exposing her bare thighs, in her typical village girl style, Claudia protested in the only way she knew she could. 'Merde. Merde. Stop it, you two, Merde!'

During her last confession at church, she had promised herself and Padre Jose never to say Merde, that word 'shit,' but Bula had provoked her. Knowing well that the best way to deal with her sisters was to leave them alone, Claudia waded back through the knee deep rain water that had engulfed her house; rains being incessant all night.

The mango tree in Claudia's frontyard gave its fruit during the monsoons. The monserrate mangoes would break and fall to the ground as the rains showered, unlike most other varieties of mangoes which ripened in summer. They were crimson and green in colour, sweet and delicious. Claudia squatted every time she felt something round beneath her feet as she waded through the water pond formed overnight by rains. She managed to collect quite a few mangoes.

Her two older sisters were supposed to join her in picking up the spoils of the heavy rains but changed their minds when they saw Damiáno. On most days, Damiáno jogged at dawn but due to the rains at night, the streets were messy; so he was simply strolling by instead of jogging. In the semi darkness of a drizzly morning, Jakin and Bula had conspired to trap Damiáno in their little ragging game. The rotten mango they aimed missed by an inch as he walked past their house.

Claudia returned home, pushed the kitchen door open and dumped the mangoes on the old kitchen table. She then quickly rushed to the river bank where Mother was gathering the floating pieces of broken palms and wood. Despite the drizzle, dim sunlight covered the riverside; village children frolicked by the banks, oblivious to their running noses and the drizzle overhead wetting them. Claudia smiled on seeing their happy faces; little girls with braided hair loops, boys in tailored shorts and shirtless chests, blowing whistles. She joined them in the common monsoon song, '*Sun and rain, the monkeys are marrying. The frogs are praying. The dogs lie at the table.*'

The rainy season had transformed Oroshim, a low lying area weathered by the warm salty breeze from the sea. Rain in Oroshim brought leaking roofs, sudden flashes of lightning and floods. They also brought some of the coveted supplies to the village; bread fruit and coconuts that fell from the trees and waited overnight to be picked up for free. Things like dried palm leaves, wooden sticks and planks good enough to use as firewood floated all across the river. Like a good perfume, fragrant white Jasmine flowers bloomed abundantly; their garlands could be sold in the market place for a fair price.

As Claudia helped Mother in holding the damp wooden sticks and logs across her chest, she felt her heart thumping in an unusual way. Something Bula had said that morning repeated in her head. For once she didn't hate Bula's comment. It made her feel like a grownup. Having been robbed in the past, of her right to feel grownup enough, with two older sisters around, both in their late twenties, still unmarried. Girls their age in Oroshim, not allowed to remain single beyond their early twenties, were already married and raising children.

The village was full of restrictions and rules. If anything overshadowed Oroshim's charm, it was the mindset of the villagers and their superstitious practices and rigidities, especially towards women, making their life tougher than it already was. Girls at Oroshim were expected to be morally upright. Of course, not every girl in the village abided by the rules; some managed to break them but were clever enough to conceal it all and appear pure before the elders. Not so Jakin. She had been unfortunate or perhaps naive would be a better word. Barely twenty when it all happened, Jakin did not know to hide her wrong to escape the village wrath. When Jakin's secret was uncovered, the village experienced something sacrilegious, that's how the priest described it and that's how Jakin became the bad part of the village crowd. She still was. Youngsters in the neighbourhood were not allowed to be friendly with her, a price she had to pay for her ignorance. No village elder considered her, when they found a prospective match like they did for other single boys and girls in Oroshim. Unfortunately, not much later, Bula went on to do something similar, giving the village an authority to categorise the two sisters as girls of bad character.

Unable to correct anything or convince the society, their father decided to numb his frustration with alcohol, and with it, his family's happiness. Claudia, the youngest of the three girls, was born twelve years after Bula, who was born a year after Jakin. Claudia grew up hating to be the baby of the house. But in the morning, when Bula drew her attention to Damiáno staring at her thighs, she liked that thought, that adult like feeling. No one at home had treated her like a grownup. Claudia wondered if they had even noticed that she was now a fully grown young adult woman. It reminded her of something she did a while back; something secretive but something that made her happy. It was when she had first started undergoing a physical metamorphosis, so to say. No one at home seemed to care or notice, each of her family members were all sucked into their own individual struggle to survive. As the days passed, the mirror surprised Claudia as she observed her breasts growing. No one at home had observed it or reacted to it. Not even Mother. Claudia felt awkward to talk to Mother about it. Instead, she decided to attend to the issue herself by taking one of Mother's old brassieres and altering it with a needle and thread to fit tight and firm. Her reflection in the mirror now brought a new look altogether. She loved it in a strange kind of way, even though it made her feel a little shy to roam openly to flaunt her new look in Oroshim, wearing her mother's altered bra.

Years back, Oroshim was just bare land, occupied only by families unable to afford their own houses elsewhere. Padre Raul, the good hearted parish priest had helped these families to settle down, build houses and supplied them with free food to make a comfortable living apart from the natural agricultural produce available at Oroshim in plenty. When he died, the people had to find their own means to survive. Free food stopped but the church continued overseeing the moral lifestyle of Oroshim's families. It was only recently that the well-to-do Portuguese family occupied the only palatial mansion at Church Square. The parish priest, Padre Jose, offered Claudia's Mother a job as domestic help there. It turned out to be a big help. Claudia's Father, who complained about things, did not object too, because of the involvement of the church.

Claudia accompanied her mother to work. She called the Portuguese lady Paklin Bai, the white Madam, in her local language. One of the reasons she loved to work in her house was because of Paklin Bai's generosity, at least with the evening snacks and used old clothes which Claudia altered and wore happily. One time; Mother and Claudia accompanied Paklin Bai to the church square field where Damiáno was playing a football match. Claudia wore Paklin Bai's altered red lacy dress, she loved the feel of the plentiful gathers the dress had at the waist but Mother somehow seemed displeased with the dress.

'You'll be better off not wearing this dress, Claudia.'

'But Mother, the dress is so pretty, why don't you like it?'

'It's not good to allow these men to stare at you.'

'Mother, why would they?' Claudia lowered her voice to ask, though startled at the faint possibility of Portuguese men staring at her. Mother clenched her teeth, a common expression of anger among the village mothers.

'Stop arguing. I am your mother. So many of those white skinned men have lured our girls, got them pregnant and gone away. And what do we do about it? Our girls are not silly, just that they get charmed with such fair and tall men. Who wouldn't? Hear it from me Claudia; those men have no limit to their bold mischief. You better be careful about them,' Mother warned, her voice stern.

'Mother, talk softly. Please.'

'Then promise me Claudia, you will never fall prey to these white men.'

'Mother, these are rich folks, and what is it that we have that we should catch their attention? We don't even have proper clothes to wear or normal food to eat in the house; I doubt you got it right Mother.'

Mother clenched her teeth and made eyes, again.

Oroshim ruins

Claudia entered through the back door; it creaked open with just one push from her. As servants at the mansion, she and Mother always entered through the backyard. Her heart leaped at the sight of Damiáno sitting alone. She really hoped he remembered her for pouring water over his feet and not for the rotten mango her sisters tried targeting him with. He turned back and mumbled something. His half bare back was towards the radio placed on the dining table; a made-in-Japan transistor that looked like a little silver box with a solid brown leather strap. Claudia remembered the time when Mother had asked Paklin Bai its price, wishing she could buy one for Father to distract him from his drinking and to keep him home at nights. When Paklin Bai told her its price, Mother never dared to think of buying a transistor radio or keeping Father home.

The song on the transistor came to an end with an abrupt quietness. Bang! The empty water pots clattered to the floor. It wasn't intentional but it did draw his attention. 'Ahh so noisy,' Damiáno said, turning the radio off and staring at Claudia with eyes narrowed. You could tell the sudden noise did annoy him.

'Nobody home?' Claudia gulped a sudden spit that welled up in her throat and swallowed it hard with nervousness as she asked.

'O *quê*? Nobody?' He narrowed his eyes again, with a sarcastic and slightly amused tone and a visible drunken expression in his turquoise blue eyes.

On the table, Claudia noticed an open half-empty bottle of liquor lying beside a wide mouth glass, half empty too and an empty quarter plate, which she assumed was for the half eaten chunk of cheese fallen on the table cloth. Claudia picked up the cheese and put it on the plate.

'Oh Busha! Why do you call me nobody?'

'Busha is my mother,' she corrected, putting on her most polite tone that failed to conceal her nervousness.

'Then, who are you my darling?' he asked, drunken, heavy eyes glaring at Claudia. He ran his eyes all over her body. His drunken stare made her think that she should keep a distance, when he looked straight at her and slurred, '*Dá-me um beijo.*' He wanted a kiss. Sudden. Direct. She had not realised how drunk he was, until then. With the radio off there was a sudden awkward silence, making Claudia feel a bit uncomfortable to be in that situation, with him, drunk. Alone. She began to make a loud noise as she started to wash the utensils, breaking the silence with the tinkling of cutlery.

Once washed, she wiped the cutlery and arranged them in the shelf, the way Paklin Bai had taught her. Paklin Bai liked her kitchen to be well organised, at all times. Bottles of strong local vinegar and imported *aceite de olive* were kept alongside the white and mustard coloured porcelain jars, used for storing dry delicacies like Bacalhau. Ladles, cooking pots and pans, a straw basket and a straw tray hung along the blue and white kitchen wall. Like in most Goan homes, a big rooster-shaped earthen jar was kept filled with water to drink.

Claudia juggled mixed emotions. Being with Damiáno alone brought her a strangely pleasant sensation. At the same time, she remembered the stern warnings from Mother and Gormai. She thought it would be okay if he wanted to hold her hand, or throw his arm around her, but a kiss? It posed the risk of taking things deeper, she thought. Worse, she did not want to ruin things like her sisters had done. She was warned of such a thing, ever so often.

'Come here,' he called out, with a playful flirting tone in his voice as he poured himself another liberal drink from the bottle after a quick gulp of the previous sip. He then began fiddling with the radio. Inside the mansion, it was only the two of them. Outside, it was even more deserted and quiet. The locals called it big house because of its palatial size. It was a colonial house painted in saffron yellow; inside walls and window sills were ivory white. The wrought iron railings were shaped into diamond, spiral, arched and cross patterns. Two large staircases on either side led to a four pillar entrance. Spiralling motifs and mosaic paintings of rich Portuguese influence adorned the walls and pillars. The big house stood in grandeur, especially in the midst of the surrounding mud houses.

Paklin Bai and her husband Senhor Ernesto de Oliveira took the house on lease from the church authorities, after which they began its renovation; a large earthen chimney replaced the old metal chimney. Artistic, curly, floral styled stainless steel window grills replaced old square shaped rusty iron ones. The garden was fenced with rosewood in fancy patterns, with freshly planted grass making a greener and fuller frontyard lawn. Multi-coloured pieces of thick broken glass were fixed on the solid compound wall, the glass pieces shimmering during day time and guarding against trespassers at night. With the masonry work still in progress, cement bags, heaps of sand and red bricks lay strewn in the frontyard. Claudia hadn't seen any labourers on her way into the mansion, she only saw trowels, chisels and hammers lying idle on a pile of bricks; the masons must have called it a day, she had assumed as she entered.

Being the only girl left eligible for marriage in the family, as per the demanding criteria of the village, well wishers in her community reminded her far too often that she was the last vestige of all that had been good in her family. Nothing had really worked out fine for them, but if she got married respectfully and settled, the family stood a chance to resurrect its lost respect, she was told.

Her gormai too had strict instructions for her, 'If any drunken man makes a pass at you, just flee. The mere sight of a woman is enough to excite a drunken man. He is like a lion that does not think before it pounces on its prey,' Gormai had warned. 'Why is that *dukon* taking you to the Portuguese house? I hear they have a grown up boy in there and you are not little any more, Claudia. I hope that *dukon* will not ruin your life, like she did with your sisters,' Gormai had ranted, her finger wagging at Mother. *Dukon*, a female pig in its original translation, was the term locals used for a disgusting woman. Claudia had never liked anyone bad mouthing Mother, least of all anyone calling her *Dukon*.

Claudia sneaked out of the kitchen, heading straight to the water well; first she filled the bath water pots in the yard, covered them and swept the backyard. Noiselessly, she entered the kitchen to fill up empty pots and jars. Damiáno wasn't there. She assumed he went to sleep. Quickly she cleared the table and washed the glass and the cheese plate he had used. The kitchen door behind her creaked and startled her.

'Mother! Is that you? So late?'

'Is Oliveira Bab in?' Mother's ever suspicious eyes widened.

'Nah. Damiáno Bab.'

'Where is he?'

Claudia silently pointed her finger upwards, in the direction of Damiáno's bedroom.

'He didn't realise you were alone, did he? I slept too long. I still have fever. I almost forgot that Paklin Bai isn't at home. When I woke up, I suddenly remembered and came rushing here, knowing you'd be alone.' Her mother said, rubbing her eyes, bulging from just waking up and a bit swollen with fever. 'He may be sleeping. I haven't seen him since I entered the mansion.' Claudia lied. She knew it was the only way she could help comfort Mother and relieve her tension.

That night, after dinner, as the ringlets of smoke from the burning oil lamp ceased, Mother, Jakin and Bula fell into a deep sleep. Claudia lay awake, fantasising on what could have happened between her and Damiáno. The continuous dripping noise of the rain was the only sound accompanying her wakefulness. This wasn't the first night she was lying down with thoughts of Damiáno dominating her mind. She had fantasised before, but tonight the thoughts were a bit more daring. Sensuous.

The next day, when Claudia went to work at the church kitchen as she did every morning, Sankistao brought up the topic of the *satyagrahis* who had come to free Goa and drive out the Portuguese. Claudia didn't like the term 'drive out.' It seemed more suited to summer flies and noisy crows, she thought. She got along well with Sankistao, the sacristan-cum-cook. His name was Abel but everyone called him Sankistao, who, apart from taking care of the sacristy and helping in the parish activities, also cooked for the church priests.

Claudia and Sankistao never ran out of things to talk about. He told her about a gut feeling he had, that someday the Portuguese would leave and Goa would belong to the Indians. He also mentioned a time when a group of *satyagrahis* had come to protest and how the rumours spread that they got beaten up.

'But they may come back, to make sure the Portuguese leave,' he said.

'I don't think the Portuguese are all that bad, Sankistao, though the young men at times get naughty, especially with our younger women.'

Sankistao laughed. 'Well, that's not the reason they have to go away, Claudia. Young men everywhere will be like that. In my opinion, there are not many young men who would not feel tempted to get naughty, especially with younger women.'

Sankistao's laughter rose higher as he repeated some of her own words, his eyes displaying a mischief that's typical of old men.

'Getting naughty with women?' Claudia questioned with an impassive look, slightly uncomfortable to hear it coming from an ageing man like him.

'Oh yes. I guess that's how young men are, Claudia. Anyway, if it's the Portuguese men that you particularly don't like, you don't have to worry much. Like I said, I am getting a feeling they may soon leave and go.'

'Do you think that "driving out" will really happen?'

'Looks like it, girl! I get this feeling that someday soon a war will break out.'

'O Sankistao, you think a war can break out in a place like Oroshim? Our Oroshim is full of order. This village has no room for either war or love. What do you have to say now?'

'Didn't you ever hear anyone say everything is fair in love and war? Similarly, war and love is fair everywhere. Wars happen. Just like Love happens.'

'Love happens?'

His talk intrigued her; love was a better topic than war. She wanted to talk more on this topic. Much older in age and experience, Sankistao knew that those were not things an older man like him should be talking with a young girl. It wouldn't go down easily if someone overheard their conversation. 'All work finished? You must leave; your mother will be waiting, Claudia.' Sankistao diverted the conversation abruptly. Claudia liked spending time with him. He was wise, clever and had a way of answering even odd questions which she could ask no one else but him; questions that Father used to patiently answer years back. Perhaps, it was one of the reasons she had begun to like Sankistao. Just like Father, he had knowledge about a lot of things and was fluent in Portuguese.

The clanking noise of a metal spoon hitting the sides of the big tin mug woke up Claudia the next morning. It was Jakin, making Mother a *masad*; hot coffee poured over a vigorously beaten egg. It was the local cure for chest congestion. The congestion subsided but Mother was still feverish with no appetite. Somebody suggested trying the jaundice remedy, a practice of burning a part of the skin, usually an area above the wrist. Half the women in Oroshim, when unwell, went around with a burn on their hand. Jakin decided to do the same for Mother.

That evening, a spoon kept for a while in the burning cooking fire was made ready for Mother. Holding the hot, scalding spoon with a cloth, Jakin placed it hastily on Mother's wrist. Bula and Claudia closed their eyes, unlike Jakin, they were a bit more sensitive to watch Mother being burnt. It was a look of fake braveness on Jakin's face, a loud terrifying squeak from Mother, and the burn, the brutal char, the ancestral remedy supposed to cleanse blood and kill infection, was done. It would take time to heal, at least a week. Until then, Mother would not be able to do any work. With Mother at home and Paklin Bai out on a short voyage, Claudia knew she would be alone in the mansion with Damiáno. Her mind hadn't stopped engaging her in strange fantasies, ever since.

Bula was lazy. Claudia was glad that she was, this time. Jakin accompanying her was also ruled out since it was a while since she had stopped visiting anyone's house, not even for work. It meant that none of her sisters would accompany her to the mansion. Late in the afternoon, Claudia went to the big house, a bit anxious, a bit afraid but excited about the uncertainty of what lay ahead. When she pushed open the kitchen door, Damiáno wasn't there in the kitchen. But she knew he was there, somewhere inside. He could have heard the noise of the vessels being washed, but he didn't come out. After almost an hour's work was done she saw him sitting in the front garden, reading. Nothing exceptional happened that day. Even when she came close to hand him a glass of water and his daily cup of tea.

The next day when Claudia entered the big house, she came wanting to make the most of the moment. Paklin Bai would be back and Mother was slowly recovering. It could be her only chance to spend time alone with him at the mansion; something she had daydreamed of in the past, and had spent until midnight longing for, the past few nights. He was in the garden reading his book when she handed him the glass of water. Their eyes met a few times. Girls in Oroshim enjoyed male attention, but they had to pretend they didn't. Claudia hated the pretence. She wished she could tell him that she liked him but she chose to remain silent. Deny it. Go with it. It was like a little war raging inside her. She saw him read the book. Close it. Shove it aside. Yawn. Look into the open emptiness of an airy afternoon. Yawn again. She could keep him engaged, she thought to herself, and wished he could only talk to her, once, before that precious window of opportunity was shut for good.

With much thought, she decided to bust a redundant silence. She looked at him right on. 'Bab, did Ti Botelho take you around the village on Sao Joao?' Claudia asked.

'*Que*?' He sounded like he was taken aback.

'Have you been around my village? Did Ti Botelho ....'

'Ah! No, no. On the day of the festival? Oh no, Botelho was in a state to only show me the wells here.' He laughed. 'But why do you ask?'

'Would you like to see our Oroshim hills?' she asked, stunned at her own boldness. He looked at her surprised. Unable to respond, he stared at her blankly, but she stared back, wishing he wouldn't decline her offer. 'It wouldn't take long, Bab,' she persisted.

'Well then, alright. Sure.'

Claudia turned quickly towards the back door and continued her work. Four trips to the water well helped her to fill the two brass pots for drinking, the earthen pots for the day's usage and the rest to wash the crockery and the cutlery. After sweeping the house, she returned to him at the frontyard garden. 'Drink it hot, it will keep you warm. It's windy outside.' Claudia said, holding a white tin mug of steaming tea in her hand. He took the mug, still surprised at her sudden talkativeness. 'Bab, you need to wear something full. It will be cold at the bunds.' She said, eyeing his broad chest under a semi-transparent cotton vest, to which he nodded, a charmed grin touching his ruddy face.

There was something about the master-maid attraction. The local girls looked up to their Portuguese Bab in admiration and respected it; could be their colour, their exuberance, their wine, their food, their flirtations or even their ability to provide good food and clothing to the servant class. The masters on the other hand found the local girls to be humble, serving them with a fervent faithfulness, hard working, and mostly attractive, face powdered white and wearing bright, feminine and frilly dresses that gave them a raw native appearance. It was because of such magnetism that it wasn't uncommon to hear about a secret seduction between a Portuguese master and a local servant girl.

Set to go up to the hills, Damiáno and Claudia walked along the red mud lanes, past the rows of datura plants, past the bougainvillea bushes and through the borom trees.

The villagers, though highly conservative on most issues involving women, had a strange logic when it came to the local women being seen with other men, including the Portuguese. Since many of the local girls and women were employed as maids with well to do Portuguese households, the elders did not mind them working or accompanying them for grocery shopping, visits to the fish market or even while going to the tailors. The maidservants were allowed to freely accompany their Portuguese masters to complete their routine chores. However, the elders had a problem when a young girl was seen with her Portuguese master if she was known to have had any illicit relationship with him.

During the Portuguese rule, there was open friendliness expressed among the Goans. Hugging and embracing a member of the opposite sex during celebrations like feasts, Christmas, weddings or New Year was done without malice.

However, there were those that yielded to a deeper physical intimacy that culminated into clandestine affairs, sometimes young girls and a married man or a house servant and their Portuguese master; these illicit relationships though often secretive were improper and solicited staunch response from the village elders, when exposed.

Claudia and Damiáno roamed freely around the hilly, deserted areas of Oroshim. Oroshim was a small village with a very close knit community, everyone knew one another, and folks met frequently and interacted at feasts, after mass at church, during the special rosary done near the village cross, during customary events like cutting of the first cloth for the bridal trousseau and at the christening of a new born baby.

Since the villagers as well as the church elders knew that Claudia worked at the Oliveira household, it was alright for Claudia to be seen with any of the members of the Oliveira family including Damiáno. There was nothing suspicious about them, not until now, neither in the minds of the villagers nor the elders of the church, not even in Damiáno's mind. The only place where malicious and sensuous desires were nurtured was in Claudia's head. She obsessed over every little thing that transpired at the big house, she constantly replayed every little incident that involved Damiáno; spending every spare moment thinking passionately about him, his look, his presence, the things he did, whether it was mundane things like reading the newspaper or a book, or the way he brought out his cycle and went out for a ride, the way their fingers brushed when he took the tea cup from her hand, his lavish smile that reflected a gracious thanks, Claudia obsessed over it all as she lay awake at home, thinking until the late hours of the night. Each morning, her first waking thought involved Damiáno and she urgently yearned to go to the big house. This obsession had begun from the time she first poured water on his feet at the well on the day of Sao Joao feast. She replayed that scene often in her mind and each recollection brought her tremendous excitement. One memory she frequently relived was the way he looked and stared at her on the day he was drunk. That particular thought evoked a strangely sensuous feeling in her which she thoroughly enjoyed. Thinking back on that day when he was drunk, she felt a nice sensation within her; a feeling she found hard to describe. Sometimes she felt like she could stay at the Mansion and do nothing but watch him than go out anywhere else where he was not there. Other than these isolated thoughts, the very mention of his name was enough to cause her heart to beat fast with excitement. She thought about him right before going to sleep and right after waking up.

Today, she had succeeded in a way to trick him into spending time with her on the pretext of being a guide, to tour around the hilly outskirts of the village.

It was quiet around the trees, unlike in winter, when the Oroshim kids chaotically hover all day for boroms. 'Look at those ant hills, Bab!' Claudia pointed out, trying to fill a speechless void. They had to cross the bunds to get to outer Oroshim, where the hills were. The bunds, a walking path in between fields, were fenced with tall coconut trees, common in Oroshim.

'Last week it was a dry spell, but looks like the rains will pour this week. Are you alright, Bab?'

'Yes. Why?'

'There are not many people in Oroshim who do not get intimidated walking these bunds during monsoon. It is advisable not to be here during heavy rains and wind.'

'And why is it so?'

'You see all those white crosses?'

He glanced around to spot quite a few white washed cross-shaped structures of mud.

'Yes.'

'They are all built in memory of those who died in heavy rains. These swaying coconut trees mean danger when strong winds blow. Unless the gods are with you, a falling tree can take away a life, Bab. It is unfortunate that it got so windy after we stepped out. Maybe we should not have come. It's August, this is expected. You know Bab, the month is usually full of lightning and storms. It uproots many coconut trees. That's why we locals call it a disgusting month, *Agosto é desgosto*, as they say.' Claudia explained in a frightened tone. She had suddenly remembered it was the first of August. With Mother unwell, Claudia working outside and Jakin doing the cooking and washing at home, they had forgotten to eat the traditional sweet-coconut-jaggery mix, which they ate every year as per the village tradition, on the first of August.

'Ah! Don't worry. We will be fine. Won't we? Look! There are still people around.' Damiáno pointed to the labourers in the field.

'The field workers are always there Bab, sunshine or rain. They are a hard-working lot. In summer they wrap a cloth to protect their heads from the heat and during monsoon, they use a *condo*. Look, some of them are already wearing it, that hood shaped raincoat you see on them, that one is hand woven with palm leaves.'

'Interesting! Everything looks fine, look they are singing. Do you know those songs?'

'Yes, those songs are in Konkani, our local language. I accompany my Gormai to the fields often.'

'You accompany who?'

'My grandmother. I call her Gormai, all the kids here call their grandmothers Gormai.'

'Sing.' He looked in her direction with half a smile, narrowed eyes, one of his classic expressions that she had come to notice lately.

'No, Bab! Not now.' She protested shyly. 'Bab, there is no way to move forward. The bund head is narrow and a fallen coconut tree has blocked the way. The only way to move ahead is to pass through the pond. Should we turn back home?'

'Is the pond deep?'

'Not really Bab.'

'Well then.'

Damiáno got into the pond first. 'Come!' He extended his hand to her. Conscious of her nice lacy red dress, the one Mother had forbidden her to wear; Claudia pulled up her skirt a bit, to avoid getting it wet. She was glad that Mother was asleep when she left home. She had planned this whole grown-up look just for him. The dress had a good fit, especially the darts at the bust seemed to highlight her rapidly maturing, feminine figure.

The pond, meant to be used just to cross over to the other side, turned into an unexpected time of getting comfortable with each other. The pond's clear water was transparent enough to see the clean sand beneath. Tiny fish; hundreds of them swimming in unison moved gracefully. As she looked at him, she realised, he wasn't a typical boring colonial master. He came across different, playing around in the water, freely, teasing her with a splash of pond water when she wasn't looking. He playfully tried to catch a few tiny fish that kept slipping through his hands. He was fun to spend time with, she thought. Her liking for him increased.

As they got out of the water after playing around for a while, Claudia looked up at the sky, filling up with dark rain clouds. 'Looks like rain.' She said, as she adjusted her folded skirt. She led the way using her experience and strong instincts, to figure out a short cut to get home and avoid getting stuck in the rains. As they walked back, she stopped suddenly and raised her arm to point to a large tree. 'Bab, if it starts to rain, we can stop under that gum tree,' she said, to impress him with her understanding and intelligence.

'As in real gum?' He questioned, walking with intrigue towards the tree. She stopped, looked up at the sky, and looked back at him with a smile. She liked the thoughts that just came to her mind. She continued smiling and took a few quick steps, running through the bush to catch up with him at the gum tree.

'That house you see, Bab, they say it belonged to Barreto's family. Barreto went to Angola while he kept his wife in her mother's house along with her son. He never returned. Anyone will be able to narrate their sad tale to you; fisher folk in the market, women in the fields, the ladies gathering at a balcao. Even men gathering over a drink at the tavern will tell you how Barreto deserted his wife and started a new family in Angola. That's bad, isn't it, Bab?'

'That is bad.' Damiáno nodded. 'Do the village people talk a lot about others doing bad things?'

'They do, Bab. They talk about everything; no one is exempted from the village talks. The villagers take special time every day to talk, well, to gossip.' She chuckled. 'One woman starts the slander and it goes on to spread in their balcao gossip, among the ladies drawing well water, the women gathering dung at hills, during the cooking time at weddings, in the fields, at the bazaar, everywhere, realising little as to how dangerous it can be for the person who is targeted. Their irresponsible chitchat has even ruined lives, Bab. As for the men they have their time of rash chatter mostly over their feni shots at the taverns. If anybody sees me around in the village with you, they will talk about me too.' She said and stopped abruptly, realising she had spoken more than she should have with a new comer in Oroshim. Trying to change the topic, she held out a handful of clay to him. 'This is clay, Bab. Touch it. During carnival, all the kids gather here to collect this.'

'Gum. Clay. Hmm.'

'Right now the clay is damp, Bab, but it is dry during the carnival. They use it in cocads; it is very simple to make cocads Bab. Just collect dry clay into the paper and seal it with gum from these seeds. Our Oroshim children make hundreds of cocads during carnival to throw at people, throwing usually at the ones they don't really like. Will you be here in Oroshim for the carnival? It's just before Lent, which would be in the month of March of the coming year.'

'Let me see. I certainly hope so Busha.'

'You must be there Bab. It's fun; everybody painting each other's faces black, then there is the carnival parade, the splashing of dark blue water, the cocads, the intruz skits and the suvanro on the last night of carnival. But if you spot anyone with cocads try to be out of their range, Bab. It hurts bad. And my name is Claudia. Busha is my mother.'

'I'm sorry. Mamma uses the name Busha so often; I somehow imagined it to be your name,' he said, giving an apologetic smile. The wind grew cold and heavy. The thoughts came back to Claudia as she hoped for it to rain like never before, right away. And as if the rains had heard her heart's plea and what transpired in her mind, the clouds burst open and torrents of rain poured down with a great loud noise and drowned every other noise around with their force. She grabbed his hand and led him in a brisk run to the nearby ruins; little thorny bushes pricking their legs, the touch-me-not plants snapping their leaves shut as they brushed through them, a pair of bandicoots, large village rats crossing their path to get into the safety of their deep dark holes. They halted and leaned on the side wall of the ruins, shielded slightly from the heavy rain. She bent down to pick up something lying on the ground. 'Porcupines live here too,' she said, proudly displaying the quill she had just picked up. 'Let's move toward the outer side; it's cleaner and safer there,' Claudia said, leading him to another side of the old ruins, the side that had a broken down half brick wall and a roof.

'You could tell from the colour of the clouds, Bab.'

'Good we rushed in here, Claudia. Thank you.'

'You are welcome Bab, and thank you for calling me by my name at last.'

'Damiáno is not known to forget the names of beautiful women,' he said, flirtingly and she instantly caught it.

'You are good with finding short cuts. Muito Bem!'

'Muito Bem to you too, Bab,' she said blushing at her own attempt to joke by repeating his words, imitating his style.

'In what way?'

'With people. You have a way with them, Bab. They like to spend time with you, to laugh with you, to do things for you. People like you a lot.'

'People?'

'Yes, Bab. People like me for instance. You have a way with people, like I just said.'

'Oh? And is that good? Bad?' The questions created room for him to flirt a bit more.

'Bab, the rain is growing heavy, move back, you'll get wet.'

'Come,' he said, firmly, as he moved back, pulling her along with him.

'*Que hora são?*'

'It must be six o'clock, Bab.' She answered, feeling heavily conscious of their closeness as they stood under the broken roof of the ruins, trying to shield their bodies from the pouring rain.

The rains seemed to be getting thicker, heavier and noisier. A momentary realisation of being in the deserted ruins, alone, with a man was making her nervous. His woollen cardigan brushed against her cheek. She took a deep breath as she got a whiff from the smell of his body. It was a strong smell of his sweat, the rain, mixed with the smell of thick cakes of pink toilet soap that Paklin Bai always wrote in her shopping list; Lifebuoy Sabao.

'Bab.' She looked at him.

'Tell me, dear.'

'Bab,' she said again.

'Are you worried about getting home?' He asked and bent down to look into her eyes. She shook her head side to side. Then opening her mouth she said, 'Bab, the other day you asked me for a kiss, it frightened me a little.'

'I ... when?'

One look in his eyes and she saw him put on an 'I-know-nothing-about-it' expression. The look in his eyes told her he really didn't remember, his drunkenness made him say it, maybe he didn't mean much of what he said that day at the mansion. His response disappointed her deeply. She suddenly felt embarrassed to be thinking of it over and over, all the while imagining the kiss was as strong on his mind as hers.

'You were drunk, Bab. I am sorry I ...'

He gave out a sudden laugh. It sounded as if he was nervous. He reached out his hand and stroked the side of her arm, gently. She looked far away into the distance, at the sky and then back at him.

'Come closer,' he said and reached out to touch both her shoulders, pulling her with a sudden force. His presence towered over her, their bodies facing each other, his eyes filled with warmth, her heart pounding. The indiscriminate thunder continued along with the raging of the heavy rains outside. Inside the ruins, Claudia became oblivious to everything around as he clutched her face in both hands and kissed her, a quick heat of blood rushing in her face. Before she could withdraw her mind from its wandering to people and rules of Oroshim, his arms were around her, as sure and hard as the continual pouring of the rain. He continued to kiss; softly at first, her reciprocative vibes tempting him to a swift gradation of intensity. The countryside rain beat hard, the wind being boisterous; a threat that could throw down trees, drown fields and even block the way through the bunds. No fear bothered her. It was her first kiss, a longing, a learning and a dream that just came alive. She breathed in within his warm grip, awed, to find herself kissing him back, with passion and skill, equal to his. They couldn't tell how long they had been intimate with each other. Then, the church bell gonged loud, awakening them almost to reality. Minutes! Half an hour!

At the sound of the Angelus bell, she stepped back, breaking loose from his arms, wiping her mouth with the back of her palm. The rain had stopped, but she had not known of it. Suddenly conscious, she looked around anxiously, wondering if anyone had passed by them.

'I must go, it's time for Angelus. Mother will be waiting.'

He stared at her in silence, watching her step out of the ruins. No girl in Oroshim stayed out when the church bell rang for Angelus, the gong being a reminder to community folks that it was time for Angelus, the daily evening prayer. Claudia waded her feet hurriedly through the rain water on the ground, turning back once to check on Damiáno. He wasn't too far behind, which called for her walking even faster; it would be bad if anyone caught them together at such a late hour, harder still, if anyone suspected that it was just the two of them at the ruins.

Claudia was reminded about the many cases involving local women and the Portuguese masters in Goa. Until now, she had not given much attention to the riskiness of the covert affairs taking place between a local maidservant and her Portuguese Bab. Now she did, on realising that in all likelihood, this is how most of the affairs started.

She was now experiencing the onset of the first beginnings. The experience of a typical housemaid doing domestic chores in a household, she and her master, alone in a large house with plenty of privacy and sometimes simply going out to assist him on an outdoor errand.

Claudia now was able to relate to some of the local servant girls who felt drawn towards the master of the house and the attractions which went on to become an irresistible force, ultimately leading to sexual intimacy. Right now however, none of the logic or attempts to justify the anxiety she faced could surpass the pleasure she felt of the reality of what just happened between her and her young Portuguese Bab. The feeling was nothing close to the happiness she had experienced ever before.

She wiped her mouth, lips, cheeks, even her neck; making sure he had not left any mark on her supple skin. Even the fragrance of his soap on her could raise suspicion, because at home they never used any fragrant soap. They always boiled soap nuts from Gormai's compound for a homemade bathing froth. Claudia reached home, panting a bit for breath; she stood with folded hands before their home altar.

Lourdina's wedding

Gormai knew of a good spot to collect cow dung—the hillock near Tukaram's farm where the cattle grazed. Claudia wished she didn't have to spend a pleasant September morning inhaling dung odour. But it was wedding time in Oroshim, and anything for a wedding, whether it was in the family or neighbourhood. It was Claudia's first cousin Lourdina's wedding. When Gormai asked her to help in cleaning the wedding house, Busha, Claudia's Mother, being the daughter-in-law of the family, had to oblige.

Blending herself in the backdrop of the early morning hillscape, oblivious to the odour that wafted across the hill, Claudia collected dung in a bamboo basket.

Fresh hill air crackled through the cashew trees and the teak wood trees.

The flooring of mud pressed houses, if ignored for a while, became flaky and dirty giving the place a shabby look. No amount of sweeping or wetting worked. Only a good, fresh coat of cow dung helped restore the clean look of the flooring. Mother and Claudia scooped handfuls of dung; spreading it patiently across the floor, meticulously. Neighbours and relatives began to arrive to help, carrying along their pre-wedding contributions; bottles filled with thick pork fat, bunches of half ripe bananas, straw baskets filled with freshly baked bread, two piglets, cut and cleaned and a sack full of rice. Claudia's attention shifted from the dung floor to the abundance of wedding provisions brought generously by folks arriving one by one.

Gormai stopped everything on seeing the church priest come to the house. '*Boa tarde*, Senhor Padkur.' Gormai greeted him a good afternoon with a respectful bow and a welcoming smile. The sight of the priest's white robes had started to stir panic in Claudia's heart, of late, with a nagging thought in the corner of her mind that her relationship with Damiáno could be exposed. So far, she had had three intimate meetings with Damiáno without anyone knowing about it.

'Senhor Padkur, since her childhood, Lourdina preferred eating in earthen bowls. Please pray that it does not rain on her wedding,' Karmin Timai was telling the priest, recollecting a common village belief that if a young girl ate in earthen vessels, it would rain on her wedding day. Claudia mumbled a silent prayer for the priest to leave; the sooner he left, the calmer she would be.

'It's nice to see Claudia helping with the wedding preparations,' Padkur said, with an observant look at all the goings on.

'Yes, Senhor Padkur, my Claudia is the best of all my grandchildren,' Gormai added with a proud, show off tone. Claudia wished Gormai would not say anything that would prolong Padkur's visit. There she goes, my old grandmother deliberately complimenting me publicly to get some work done, Claudia whispered in her mind, looking at Gormai with a knowing grin.

'I agree with you on that point, Claudia is certainly one of the best young girls in Oroshim. The girl is growing up so fast and it won't be too long before we have to announce the wedding banns. Keep the bird in the cage lest it flies in the wrong direction. What do you say Busha?' the priest said with a casual smile, his remark making her heart begin to thump. A sudden fear ran over her as a curious question arose in her mind. 'Do they know?'

It was when the church worker emptied the big sack of coconuts in the kitchen, Claudia knew the priest had come on behalf of the church elders with a wedding gift of hundred coconuts, and it was nothing concerning her. Phew! She could have blown the loudest whistle in excitement.

Gormai continued assembling more folks to help out. Claudia was always excited about weddings; wedding music, wedding food, the wedding decorations, the wedding ceremony, it all fascinated her. She thoroughly enjoyed watching happy faced bridal couples stealing shy glances and proudly holding hands in public. She was intrigued to think how it was possible for even ordinary people to look so beautiful and happy on their wedding day.

The fresh dung would dry up by the time guests arrived in the evening for *roce*, the ceremony where the bride would be cleansed with coconut milk to be ready for her big day. It would take plenty of coconuts to get the right amount of extract, which would suffice for relatives and neighbours gathered for the *roce* ceremony. The neighbouring ladies came, along with their coconut graters, to sit in a line in the backyard. Some of the men energetically dehusked coconuts with sharp iron choppers, some others breaking the peeled coconuts. They whistled tunefully, sharing amused laughter among themselves as they ragged the women sitting at a near distance to grate the semi circled kernels flawlessly. All the grated coconut was then ground to a thick paste, strained through a thin cloth to a thin consistency of milk, readied for the bride. The coconut milk was placed in large bowls and set before the bride who sat on a low wooden stool, the bridesmaid sitting beside her. Then, accompanied with traditional songs one person at a time would take a portion of the milk and dab it on the bride's head as well as her face, neck and hands while also applying a small portion on the bridesmaid. The pre-wedding events always stirred an air of jubilance. It was a time of coming together. Old grudges were suddenly overlooked. Everyone worked together in the preparation and customary events leading to the wedding.

Claudia and Mother participated in the preparations. Bula spent some time and left as soon as she got a chance to pull some pink streamers from the wedding decorations. The sisters would dip the pink crepe paper in water and rub it on their lips as the paper released a purple pink colour to offer a nice magenta effect. It was the only make up used, apart from face powder, for special occasions.

Post sunset, the *roce* ceremony began. From the closest family members down to the neighbours, the *roce* went on in the backdrop of folk songs and blessings. Older folks were good with the traditional *roce* ceremony songs, blessing the bride and her loved ones through their folklore. Karmin Timai passed around *lathod*, rice cake made with coconut and jaggery, a common sweet. Cashew feni was served to the men. The singing went on even after the girl's last bath in her mother's home. 'No need to envy Lourdina, you will make a beautiful bride, if only you don't play around like your sisters,' Gormai started the preaching that she often annoyed Claudia with, especially within the hearing of her mother and sisters.

'Who's envious of Lourdina? Not me, at least,' retorted Claudia with confidence. 'And well, I certainly won't play with my life like ....' she was cut off before she could complete the sentence.

'Won't happen with words alone. Takes will power to say no to temptation. When my eyes are still open, I want to see you settled well Claudia,' Gormai taunted, slanting a sly glance at Mother.

'Oh Gormai, why do you talk like that?' Claudia questioned as her thoughts once again went back to the lingering doubt in her mind, 'Does she know anything about me and Damiáno?'

The speakers set up by a local wedding supplier burst out with loud music in the tent set up in front of Lourdina's house on the wedding morning. It was Gormai's house which was also Claudia's Father's ancestral house. However, since Claudia's family did not live there nor were welcomed as they should have been, they could not call it their house. Only on occasions like weddings, funerals and feasts, they gathered together as one family.

Father sat sober in church. He had not drunk all day; he wore his old grey suit over a white-turned-bluish-with-indigo shirt. The wide purple printed tie that was lying unused in their old wooden almirah for years now hung over his chest reaching down below his belly button. The bridegroom's party occupied one side of the pews, while the bride's people occupied the other. Claudia's family was made to sit on the third pew, Gormai squeezing in to sit beside Claudia.

The choir began to sing at the Senior Priest's entry and the nuptials began. All heads turned to the main door to glance inquisitively at the bride and groom and the congregation stood up in respect.

'Look at Father, looking even smarter than Lourdina's groom.' Claudia whispered to Gormai with an amused smile. The remark instantly got Gormai straining her neck to look at her son, nodding in agreement. The look on Gormai's face reflected pride to see her son sitting sober and neatly dressed for the occasion.

Jakin was yawning; she wouldn't be the only one waiting for the nuptials to get over. There would be others just waiting to get out of the church and reach the venue of the wedding reception. Bula fidgeted and fiddled with her dress and her hair, looking around. Desperate to get some male attention. Mother sat with a proud expression. It was very rare that she came out all dressed up and feeling grand, sitting beside her husband.

The priest's voice echoed loudly in the stillness of the church. 'Two are better than one.' He was quoting the holy book from the high altar. Is that what is written in the holy book? If it did, she'd love the book. Does God think two are better? Two as in: she and Damiáno. Her mind wandered off as she began to dream of him marrying her. Sudden memories of things that happened under the gum tree flashed across her mind. Church was not the place to allow such thoughts. She knew it well. Would it anger the Lord? That's the way they threatened her when she was a child. They'd point out to the big eyed picture of Jesus at the altar in Gormai's sitting hall, mostly when she and her sisters were caught doing something mischievous 'Look, Jesus is staring at you,' they would frighten them. It worked then, though she wished the painter had not painted such big eyes for Jesus on that painting.

The sermon went on. However, many looked forward to what lay ahead: fun, dance and gaiety of a wedding celebration, that carried a promising potential to change people's moods almost magically in the village. Claudia's gaze shifted to Father seated to Mother's left. Father's expression was a little hard to read, but a subtle smile seemed likely to break out on the creases of his thin face, which was otherwise either morose or drunken with a funny droop at the chin. He looked engrossed witnessing the wedding nuptials, making an effort to sit through the rituals. His willingness to remain sober since morning was proof enough about the reverence people of the village showed towards a wedding day.

At the time of the wedding reception, there was no trace of rain. The ground was well watered, levelled nicely for dancing. The combination of paper ribbons, palm leaves and multicoloured balloon decorations on poles made the place look jubilant. The gramophone played melodious Konkani songs, couples stood by to join in the wedding march. The unmarried men approached young women to invite them on the dancing floor. A young man from the bridegroom's side requested Claudia for a dance, she obliged on getting that non-verbal nod of approval from Mother. Another young man from the groom's side approached Bula for a dance. Bula obliged too. The man wasn't much of a looker. He appeared a bit older and balding; an unmarried oldish man or a widower it seemed like. But Bula was very happy, smiling ear to ear as she danced with him.

Jakin, on the other hand, was helping out, trying to be a part of those women who were not a part of dancing. The others, either too old to dance or shy to step on the dancing floor publicly, were engaged in helping out in the kitchen or in serving. They were mostly aging women and none as young as Jakin. But Jakin was still happy working alongside those women in the kitchen. Though she wasn't a part of dancing, she still had a merry smile on; happy and dressed apt for the occasion, like most participants at the wedding.

The atmosphere was happy. Merry-hearted. Buoyant. Forgiving. Lively. The entire village of Oroshim seemed to have come together as one big family, soaking in the joyfulness of a neighbourhood wedding. Rice pulao was served after a few rounds of dancing, each plate with a topping of boiled diced carrots, potatoes and green peas. Glasses of lemonade were passed in large wooden trays. Kids gulped down the first glass quickly and clumsily grabbed a second glass, spilling some of the liquid and messing the floor. A round of chilled beer glasses were passed to the men.

Though the wedding celebration was over before midnight, *shim* had to be done, a customary division between the groom's people and the bride's. The first day of wedding always ended with the thick line of fermented local drink poured on the street separating folks from both the sides. Men sang wedding folk songs with loud, drunken-sounding voices, they seemed to have the vigour to stay awake all night to sing and continue with the celebrations. Children got cranky and dull with sleep, women yawned in tiredness, but no one complained or showed any interest to wind up the celebrations or go home. Though it was nearing midnight, everyone was happy to stick around, as was common at most weddings in the village. The women talked and laughed and got along well with each other, while the men continued to drink and enjoy the last custom of the day, the *shim*.

The next morning, despite being awake until late night, the neighbourhood women gathered early to start the preparations of the second day of wedding. The second day, as customary in Goa, was a time to host the bridegroom's people at the bride's place. The day's work was allotted and the women formed groups of fours and fives to get each chore going; cleaning, grating, grinding and everything that went into the making of the second day's dinner menu. It included delectable dishes like Galinha cafreal, country fowl xacuti, sausage pulao made with pork fat, meat vindaloo, green beef curry, beef roast and sorpotel. Claudia was in the group that was to prepare sorpotel. The older folk called it sarapatel; an ancient and unique dish prepared with pork meat, fresh blood and offal. The Portuguese carried the sarapatel recipe to many parts of the world that they colonised. It was said that the African slaves in Brazil were the first ones who thought of adding offal to the recipe; unusual parts of the pig like pig tails, feet, intestine, tongue and ears; the probable waste which the slave masters discarded. This story fascinated Claudia, even though she wasn't sure how far it was true.

One of the ladies assumed the responsibility to take charge of the cooking. She dropped all the required ingredients into a large basin. Claudia sat down behind the heavy grinding stone, and began churning the thick stone in slow circular motion, adding the spices one by one as the stone crushed them with each round motion, as granite rubbed against granite with a rough gravelly noise mixed with the soft squishing sounds of the crushing spices; long, dark red dry chillies were the first to go in along with a sufficient amount of water, then, black cloves, sticks of cinnamon, cumin seeds, pepper corns, turmeric, tamarind and a bit of sugar. Once the above spices were all crushed and ground, chopped onions were added which now began to make the concoction turn slushy and thick. To this she added pieces of skinned ginger and garlic flakes. She then added some vinegar and continued mixing until the entire mixture turned smooth. Grinding the sarapatel spice mix took Claudia a little over half an hour. Meanwhile someone else diced the meat and cut the other organs which was parboiled in advance and set aside to cool down. Once Claudia was done with the grinding she was then instructed by the cooking in charge to fry the diced meat, adding the ground masala to the meat to stir fry it for a few minutes. When the coconut feni and fresh pig's blood, heated and thickened, was added with a few pinches of salt, sarapatel, the prime dish, was done. Although it seemed to be one of the more laborious dishes to prepare, it was a pièce de résistance among other dishes, which would be served with freshly baked sannas, the toddy soaked rice cakes.

Nearly half the village would be attending the celebration, apart from the main guests of the evening; the bride and groom's family, friends and relatives along with the newlyweds. Preparing food for the second day celebration took a lot of work. The momentum picked up with everyone eager to help, making sure everything was ready before the guests arrived.

In between all the happenings, the ladies never stopped talking. Curious talks with a bit of badmouthing was a typical part of most wedding discussions. People from the groom's side took pleasure in finding fault with the bride's and the bride's folk retorted with gossip about the groom's people. Some of the discussions led to loud, animated arguments. The animosity and arguing would end only when the celebrations and customs were done.

Claudia wasn't interested. She had other things to worry about. At the moment, she could think of nothing else but wish that all the attention and merriment happening for Lourdina's wedding would happen for her family too. That would be the day. Wedding bells chiming for her. She imagined Father wearing his suit and tie again, shoulders straight, head high, with a proud father-of-the-bride expression, going around bragging. Her mind wandered to loudspeakers blasting out love songs in her frontyard. People bringing gifts. Lots of hustle and bustle with everyone running around doing things for her too, just like they did for Lourdina. She pictured the long trail of her immaculate white gown that would sweep through the floors of her house as she stepped out gracefully, then across the church entrance and inside the church through the nuptials, and later, the white trail would tread the dance floor of the wedding reception venue. And as she danced, she could feel everyone's eyes on her as her ears filled with the cheers of everyone around.

'Claudia, stop dreaming girl, there are plates to be washed and dried. Go, hurry.' Gormai's sudden shout shook Claudia out of her beautiful daydream.

Tomorrow, before dawn

Claudia and Mother had been at the local furnace, baking small round cakes until early morning, after which they went to Gormai's house where the cakes had to be counted and arranged in large baskets along with equal number of bananas to be sent, as per local custom, to the bridegroom's house. At last, all the work to do with the wedding customs was done. It was nearing 4:00 pm, when they left for the mansion, after an absence of four days at work.

Light pink nerium, double shaded hibiscus, yellow chrysanthemums, red roses, orange abolim and white jasmine brightened up Paklin Bai's garden but it was the punctual blooming of the four o'clock flowers that always drew Claudia's attention as soon as she entered the mansion. In some way, they reminded her of the time when she was a little girl. In those days, Mother would teach the girls to make garlands from the four o'clock flowers. It was a time when all the women in the neighbourhood were together, as one team, as one big family and were always available to help one another with anything including cleaning the fish, preparing evening snacks, weaving palm fronds, making pickle. Those days their gossip centred only on anyone indulging in something that was controversial or taboo. A girl getting engaged to someone from Bombay but was later deserted without marriage. A married woman spending time talking to another man while her husband was at sea, working on the ship. A boy whose real father was a Portuguese man and not the one his mother married. A woman who attempted a remedy to cure her alcoholic husband by squeezing fish head in his drink, and the husband died of food poisoning which made the village throw her out.

All sorts of gossip was entertained at the balcao. But it was the giggling and laughing that drew the women together the most. The silliest of jokes could spark off peals of continuous laughter and the same joke would be repeated by different women to elicit a fresh round of laughter over and over again. The balcao also converted into a counselling centre; women openly wept, expressing their frustrations about a previous night's argument with a husband or a mother-in-law.

Gormai's balcao, in those days, was a much sought after, welcoming place, large enough to accommodate many Oroshim ladies. The mothers chatted while the daughters played hopscotch with broken pieces of country tiles. Often, women would gather the young girls to oil the girls' hair and clean up their nits, not just their own daughter's; they treated all the girls as their own. It was at the balcao that the fruit and vegetable vendors took a halt to relieve themselves from the day's tiredness. A place where they would be happy to lower the basket of unsold merchandise from their head and relax. The wide straw basket which was skilfully balanced on their head as they moved from house to house, *waddo* to *waddo*, and village to village, with loud shouts of beans-brinjal-gourds to announce themselves to the housewives.

At the balcao, it was their opportunity to destress, to discuss things on their hearts with openness, to learn a few secrets from the more experienced women like Gormai who had much wisdom and experience in managing life, house, finances. Also, she was relied on for her sound and fair advice by those who had a quarrel with a husband or with their in-laws, concerning a marriage match, sickness, local traditions and customs or concerning almost every situation possible. The women always felt welcomed at the balcao as they exchanged warm looks and got to spend time bonding over womanly chatter. These exclusive ladies meetings were something all the village women looked forward to with excitement.

Sadly, the situation changed for Claudia's Mother when her balcao acquaintances learnt about Jakin's involvement with a man she was not supposed to be involved with. And later Bula's. What hurt Mother most was the sudden change in attitude and the way the women began treating her, with raw indifference that gradually turned into abject neglect and an unwillingness to offer any support to cover the shame she felt. And such treatment coming from women she considered to be her soul sisters caused more agony.

Golden streaks from the setting sun shimmered on the mansion walls and roof. Claudia, thrilled to be back at the mansion, ran her fingers fondly across the four o'clock flowers in the backyard. A little ahead was a heart throbbing sight; Damiáno oiling his bicycle chain. The moment he saw Claudia, he gave her a subtle smile. Claudia's heart skipped a beat on seeing him, she was too nervous to smile back and continued walking towards the kitchen, controlling her emotion. She entered the kitchen and came out in a while with the water pot to draw well water, hoping to see Damiáno again, but he was gone.

In the days that followed, she did her best to get noticed by him. Occasionally, she got a look or a flirtatious smile from him, sometimes a brief eye to eye. She wanted more. Things that happened between the two of them, near the gum tree, at the ruins went on to become hauntingly prominent in her heart and mind. By now she had sensed in her heart that whatever happened between them was not just a onetime master-servant intimate encounter. The way she felt about him ever since, it had to be more than that.

In the mornings, when she woke up, her first thoughts were of Damiáno. His face was imprinted on her mind with an inerasable intensity. He was in her thoughts constantly. Dominated them almost ceaselessly. As she walked to the mansion, as she went about doing the chores at the mansion, everything had an essence of Damiáno. The thick brownish yellow straw broom she used to sweep the back and front yard, a soft cloth to rid the rocking chair of fine dust, the watering of the garden plants, the rough husk with which she sparkled the mansion floors or the overflowing water pots as she drew bucket after bucket from the deep well in rigorous, rhythmic motion which she began to enjoy in spite of her arms aching with the exercise. Often, she was able to ignore the physical pain, with Damiáno on her mind. Everything she did was done with Damiáno on her mind and she wanted to excel. She gave herself wholeheartedly to each task, no matter how mundane. She wanted to please him, and in pleasing him, was her pleasure. Using a thick, hard soap she washed his clothes over the large rectangular, rough piece of red rock, used as a washing stone; shirts, trousers, handkerchiefs and vests. She took extra effort during the final rinse to get refills of fresh, clean water. Twisting the garments strongly to squeeze the water out, before drying them diligently over a long rope tied on the roof. Sometimes when Mother or Paklin Bai got occupied around the time he bathed, she got a chance to hand him a towel at the end of his well-side bath. This little act brought her unexplainable joy and she looked forward to it with great excitement.

Everything seemed special, because of his existence at the mansion and more because of his presence in her life as he occupied her heart and mind. With each passing day, her gratitude towards the ordinary chores that provided her access to his personal space and belongings increased; the beautiful white bed linen he used, the hand painted porcelain tea cup his lips touched and the sweaty stylish clothes he threw into the laundry basket. She enjoyed the pleasure of holding them for a few extra moments as she breathed in his odour that emanated from everything he seemed to touch.

At times his thoughts flooded her mind with an intensity that was almost overwhelming. During such times, she allowed her mind to wander into a world of fantasy; the copper vessels turned into a choir and broke into a melodious song. The crystal bowl and the wine glasses danced away with the spoons and ladles. The kitchen filled with the sound of a beautiful love song from the water pitcher, an inspired poem arose from the oil simmering on the pan filled with fresh *Rissois de camarao.* Sprinkles of love dust splashed out of the salt as it savoured Baffado de Galinha; a common dish in the mansion kitchen. The string of red spicy chouricos wriggled happily. Oh! How Claudia loved the dinner time at the mansion, when the Oliveira family took their seats by the beautifully carved rosewood table. It was a time of joyfully serving her masters and her mistress, which had turned into a time of silent glances, stolen smiles, major vibes exchanged and gentle little touches which no one else noticed except Claudia and Damiáno.

Mother, busy in the kitchen, Oliveira Bab engrossed in the newspaper, Paklin Bai concentrating on her son's food; all of it allowing Claudia an opportunity to gain Damiáno's attention to herself. 'Claudia, pass the salt. Claudia bring the cloth napkin. Claudia serve Damiáno Bab some soup,' Paklin Bai's orders were relentless even as she relished her food. Waiting at the dinner table, Claudia served with a happy smile all the while sensing strongly the junior Bab's vibes. A gentle nod of his head proclaiming a non-verbal thanks from Damiáno, his naughty half smile with a mischievous wink. So much happened between them both as she passed him the salt or served him a second helping or carefully poured water to wash his hands when he was done or as she held out a hand towel.

Once the monsoon had come to an end, Paklin Bai wanted the garden to be cleaned of unwanted weeds, dry shrubs and other plants that had grown. Mother and Claudia started the job. Before it got dark, the entire compound had to be cleaned and the fallen leaves had to be removed. Paklin Bai sat on her rocking chair and supervised their work, hurling out instructions on the way she wanted it to be done. She was always exact about how she wanted things. If things had to be done in a certain way, it had to be done, no excuse, no deviation. Mother lit up a fire at the corner of the compound to burn the dried leaves and weeds. Later, the ash would be used to clean the utensils.

While sweeping one side of the mansion, Claudia felt something peck her head; it was usually crow shit that targeted people's heads. Claudia looked up and saw no crow, then lowered her head to look at the ground. It was a rolled up piece of paper. She looked up at the window and saw Damiáno standing in the veranda overhead, staring in her direction, pointing to the paper he had thrown. Looking around nervously, she bent down quickly, picked the paper and tucked it quickly inside the left cup of her bra. This was the village women's way to hide something important, usually money. After gathering the last bucket of dry leaves and weeds and throwing them into the bonfire, she pulled out the paper slowly, careful to make sure no one was watching.

'Tomorrow. Before dawn. Under the gum tree.' Her fingers trembled with nervousness and her heart was beating fast as she breathed heavily and looked up at the window. He was gone. She squeezed the paper hard and crumpled it. She had to make it disappear before anyone could see the writing on it. She aimed at the burning leaves and threw the paper in and watched it until it lit up and burned.

Money for Father

'Gormaaaaii!' Claudia called out while standing outside her grandmother's house. It was still dawn. Partly chewed guavas were strewn on the ground, half eaten by bats at night. Claudia selected one that looked ripe, juicy. She was told that the bats have a knack of choosing the best guavas to eat. Lucky for her this one was barely eaten. She wiped it vigorously using her skirt, carefully took a big bite around the part that was bat-bitten, spat that piece out of her mouth with force and gorged on the rest of it, relishing every bite as she waited for her grandmother to accompany her to the seashore.

They were going to the fishermen to get a portion of the day's catch. Gormai did it for the priests. It was her way of serving the ordained elder men of her church. At times, she would select the choicest of fish available with the fishermen, clean it carefully and painstakingly prepare her most delicious curry before taking it to the local priests. Oiled hair twisted into a loose bun, a greyish black cotton sari deeply tucked at the navel, barefooted, Gormai walked towards Claudia holding a handkerchief in one hand and a netted bag in the other. Claudia held two.

Gormai was popular for treating the fishermen's children when they had worms in their stomachs. A few strong puffs of burning rolled up tobacco leaves from her homemade *Idi* into the infected child's nostrils always brought healing. Gormai's strong smelling rolled up tobacco leaf was just one of her secret remedies. Her cousin in Bombay called it a beedi, which was also the term actually used for the poor man's cigar or cigarette. The Goan locals called it *Idi.* Because of Gormai's willingness to help worm infected children and the reverence the village had for the church priests, the fishermen never refused to oblige Gormai with a portion of fish.

Holding Gormai's hand whenever the road got a bit rough, Claudia helped her walk through the beach road as the wind swept across heavily that morning. A crossing cat suddenly halted their brisk walk. It had crossed their path almost too fast to notice in the early morning darkness. Instinctively, Claudia knew that a cat had just passed in front of them, a black cat. But she chose to pretend not to have seen it, hoping also that Gormai had not noticed the cat. It would be fine if it was a rat, a porcupine, a dog or anything else, but a black cat. The whole village detested it. A black cat crossing someone's path was a bad omen. It was common to turn back if one had set out on an important task believing that the work would never get done. Worst, it was believed that it would bring bad luck and lead to negative results.

'We are almost there.' Claudia gasped, between deep breaths, still hoping Gormai hadn't noticed the black cat crossing.

'I don't think we should proceed, didn't you see that black cat?' Gormai asked firmly. She stopped abruptly and turned around to go back. Claudia remained quiet. Stunned with disbelief about how an old woman who complained of blurry eyesight could have the alertness to catch a fast moving cat in the semi-darkness of the early morning. Thoroughly irritated about having to turn back, she angrily shooed and threw a stone into the bushes where the cat seemed to have gone. She could not accept the fact that it was just an ordinary village cat that was responsible for the emptiness of their bags.

Back home, Claudia helped herself to a generous bowlful of rice kanji. It was something she relished although it was one of the simplest foods. She thoroughly enjoyed it accompanied with ample amounts of raw mango pickle.

She was a bit surprised to see Father awake early, as she ate the early morning breakfast. She noticed that Father had opened about four to five tins lying in the kitchen from the dozen Farex tins that a migrant family with whom Mother worked for a while had given which were now used for storing the sea salt, pepper, kokum, other dry masalas and all the other cooking stuff including other ingredients which only Mother knew of. Mother also used those very tins to hide whatever little money she could.

Father was not supposed to find it. Mother was clever and always came up with secret areas to hide money from Father. Many times she herself would reveal the location of the money to him out of pity to watch him get desperate to have a drink. Father found one coin in one of the tins, which must have motivated him to look into the other tins. He went on until he looked into every container in the cooking area. Unfortunately he had failed to find any more money there.

The thick polythene tablecloth not replaced or taken off for years stuck to the wooden table as if it was a part of the table itself. With his skinny arms, Father tried lifting the tablecloth; another secret hideout for Mother's money. Unfortunately, no money was to be found there too.

The solid iron box stuffed with simmering dried coconut shells was now placed by the side of Father's cot. His clothes which were to be ironed were piled up in one corner of the cot. It was a long time since Father had last worn those work clothes; the clean white full sleeves shirt and the dark grey pleated trousers.

'He said someone called him to offer a job, it is not yet confirmed, it seems they want to meet him once before making a decision. The problem is that there is absolutely no money in the house for him to travel to that place. Do you know of any money lying anywhere around the house?' Mother enquired softly. Whispering was her usual way of communicating when Father was around, which made her talks sound like she had a secret to withhold when there wasn't any.

'I think Father found just one coin in the tins,' Claudia answered, her voice soft.

'Oh, that's not enough to travel so far. He has to travel to Panjim. It's an up and down journey to travel by a caminhao, then he will need some money for his tea and snacks.'

In an attempt to find some money, Claudia had explored every possible place around the house; Father's trousers left for washing, Mother's special occasion dress pockets, under the table cloth, inside each of the masala tins. Nothing so far. Sometimes, they got money by selling a fowl or two, but the chicks in the coop were still small to be sold.

Outside in the backyard, Bula was shaking the guava tree, dropping many unripe little guavas in her bid to drop a good one. Claudia had to make a desperate choice. She chose to try and convince Bula to accompany her to the fishermen's huts by telling her about how she and Gormai returned with empty bags after seeing the black cat cross their path. She wanted to convince Bula that they could trick the fishermen that Gormai has asked for fish for the priests, which they could then sell. Deep inside she knew it would be a sin she couldn't get away from confessing at church. It had been a while since she or any of her family had been to the confession box. The mandatory confessions were due only during Lent, and there was a long time for that she thought to herself trying to justify her planned action. At that moment all she could think of was that Father was in need of money.

'A black cat crossing the path is bad. Don't waste my time, I am not coming,' Bula protested.

'Father needs money. If we go to the fishermen and tell them Gormai has asked fish for the priests, we can sell it and give Father the money.'

'Bad idea! He'll come home drunk more. Are you ready for the drama?'

'Please don't talk like that about Father, Bula. At least he is trying. If we don't arrange money for his transport, he can't go to the office; it is very far from Oroshim.' Claudia persisted. Bula gave Claudia a strange look, made an angry face and began walking reluctantly beside her.

'Gormai is too cunning. She always does things that turn out right. Its early morning and the first thing you have seen is a black cat, I doubt your silly plan will work, Claudia. I don't even think the fishermen will have any fish to give us. Let's go back,' blurted Bula.

'Why do you want to ruin things for Father?'

'I ruin things?'

'We're almost there, Bula. Now listen, I'll be telling them that the fish is for the priests, the fishermen always give good, fresh fish for the priests. So in case they ask, we tell them we are taking the fish to give it to Gormai who is not feeling strong enough to walk all the way today. Is that clear Bula?'

'Wait a minute. Why should we come all the way here and give the fish to Gormai. She may be nice to you and Father but she has always been rude with me, Jakin and Mother.'

'Bula, we won't give the fish to Gormai or the priests, it is what we are going to say to the fishermen. We just have to pretend.'

'Ah! So you mean cheating. Now I get it!' exclaimed Bula with a wicked grin. Possibly happy to get the opportunity to get Claudia into a trap which could allow her to blackmail her if required in the future.

'Whatever you think, Bula. I am doing this for Father. Please! Just help me.'

'On one condition. Actually two. If they say they don't have fish to give, you are not going to plead with them.'

'Of course I won't plead. And what is the sec ...?' Claudia suddenly controlled herself from asking the second condition.

There was no way you could trust Bula and her illogical, trifling demands.

The sun was rising across the horizon and had cast a faint reflection on the sea when they reached the seaside. Most boats were anchored and the ones that had managed a big catch were busy with the task of clearing the boats and the nets of the fish. Some were packing up. Some boats were being pulled up ashore. Claudia and Bula walked towards the boats where they observed the nets were being washed. 'No fish. Come tomorrow,' the fishermen said, when Claudia requested them to share some of their fish.

'Please, don't send us back empty. We can help in separating the fish and spreading the small ones for drying on the mats for you and we will help in cleaning the nets too,' implored Claudia with desperate urgency. 'Gormai is waiting and has already prepared the masala for the fish, the priests will be looking forward to the food,' Claudia maintained the pleading, ignoring Bula's first condition.

It worked. The pleading, the suggestion of helping in separating the multitude of fish and much needed help in washing up the absolutely soiled nets, the fishermen agreed.

Once the job was done they told the girls to pick up fish from baskets that were yet to be packed to be transported to the fish market.

Quickly, Claudia ransacked the baskets and stuffed her netted bags with as many fish she could accommodate. But in spite of the rushed job, she was making sure to hunt for the ones which could garner a better price and ignore the others.

When she thought she had enough, she hurriedly thanked the fishermen, not wanting to give them an opportunity to check how much and what kind of fish she had picked and quickly started walking by pulling Bula alongside her and left to go straight to the market.

'I see Sole fish. Pomfrets. Seer. Milk fish. Mackerels. Sardines.' Bula exclaimed, looking at the bulging bags.

'I see money,' Claudia replied.

'How much money?'

'Enough for Father to return, after meeting the senhors at the faraway office.'

'What about me?' Bula snapped, least interested in what Claudia was concerned about.

Claudia deliberately ignored her. She got busy checking the fish in the netted bags. Lots of little milk fish, good sized Pomfrets, Seer fish. Sole fish and some more. She knew the Pomfrets would fetch more money, a sigh of relief and excitement escaped her mouth as the calculations began in her mind.

'That's a lot of fish, despite the black cat,' Bula said.

'Black cat, oh yes,' Claudia exclaimed proudly with a victorious smile.

The bazaar came alive each morning with eager buyers crowding the market. Stalls, big and small, sold things on both sides of the narrow lanes. The potter advertised his earthenware with loud shouts '*Maytti*! *Thouli*! *Gurguret*.' Tamarind sellers neatly piled up mounds of tamarind sprinkled with rock salt to create more effect. The red chillies and spices piled up in neat jute bags added to the mood. The varied smells, sights and sounds mesmerised the crowd as they loitered lazily from stall to stall, stopping to inspect everything on display. But not really purchasing much. Just enjoying fantasising about the taste and relish of the ingredients being cooked up as they continued to look out eagerly for something at a special bargain. The flower sellers attractively lined up their hand woven garlands of aromatic flowers. Vegetable vendors sprinkled water on their neatly arranged heaps of vegetables on large baskets filled with fresh produce from the fields. The fragrance of flowers died down and an overwhelming fishy stench filled the air as Bula and Claudia reached the salt fish stalls where the sellers began to set up their merchandise.

Unable to bear the strong smell, Bula made funny faces and murmured and kept rubbing her nose. As they moved on further the overpowering unpleasant smell began to subside, gradually receding as the smell of freshly boiled beef soup, oven baked rissois, croquettes and chourice pao took over.

A trip to the bazaar was a way of life for the locals, which involved allocating dedicated time of the day. For many, the bazaar was also a place reserved to get updated with the latest happenings and had turned into a catching-up-with-folks and the latest news place, where there were energetic exchanges of various happenings; who's marrying whom and when, moments of sentimentality for those who lost loved ones, learning of special challenges recently experienced by some families, as well as the joys and almost every incident to occur between the last bumping into each other, narrated with enthusiasm at the bazaar. Tarle. Bangdde. Bombil. Peddi. Palu. Muddosheo. Lepo.

Sangott. Isvonn. Shinnaneo. Kalvam. Pilo. Mannkeo. Teesrio. Surgutteo. There were all kinds of fish available for every taste and budget. Those who could not afford the more expensive varieties drew comfort from just observing them being selected by the rich buyers and watched in mouth watering awe at them being cut and cleaned meticulously by the vendors. Sardines. Mackerels. Bombay Ducks. Hilsa. Perch. Lady fish. Sole fish. Cat fish. King fish. Mussels. Oysters. Shark. Squids. Clams. Pomfrets. Fish everywhere on this side of the bazaar.

The buyers would halt at the vendor on spotting their favourite fish. 'How is it given?' they'd ask, it was a clichéd question in the local language, and if paraphrased it simply meant 'How much?' A couple of buyers would team up to bargain over a large fish like King Fish, share the cost of it together and take home equal portions of it.

Workers were still moving fish from the straw baskets and arranging them in order over blocks of ice, covered with husk to keep them fresh. The fisherwomen readied themselves to take on the vendor's seat unconsciously and carelessly flaunting their unique look which made it easy to spot them among all the other vendors as fisher folk; a typical Oroshim fisherwoman was smooth skinned, with a body structure that was heavier than most other women. She had sharp eyes and rough black hair. Common among them was a colourful long flared skirt tied low at the waist, deep necked contrasting half sleeved blouse carrying some sort of strain to cover strong arms and a usually large bosom, a thick gold chain; sometimes two in differing designs, slung around the neck. Their hands usually tinkled a mix of pure gold and multicoloured glass bangles. A typical fisherwoman was energetic and flamboyant. Extremely sweet and loving with those who were good to her or else arrogant and loud mouthed, especially with those buyers who annoyed her with hard bargaining. She would yell at them even from a distance. Somewhat manly in the way she displayed her physical strength which almost matched her well-built physique. Not many would risk messing with her, if anyone did anger her, right at the fish bazaar, she had no hesitation in even hurling a fresh mackerel or a mullet right across, to target the person, as a means of self defence and if the argument got intense.

'That's enough. Stop it or else I will throw a mackerel at you,' she would threaten.

However, beneath that heavy and brash exterior, she usually carried a clean and kind heart. As far as selling was concerned she was resourceful, making sure the hand stitched cotton bag tied to her waist, brimmed with money at the end of the selling.

'Oh Bab, come come, fresh catch of the day. Come,' She would entice the rich men, the potential daily buyers, as she would open the fish gills to reveal the redness of the inside of the fish, the usual way a fisherwoman would try to prove that a fish is fresh.

One such fisherwoman was Magdalen, the one that eagerly waited for Paklin Bai, to come and buy her fish. Obviously, Paklin Bai's single purchase was almost as equal to ten local buyers put together, in terms of the final cost of the expensive varieties of fish purchased in spite of the smaller quantity. And the profit margin against the expensive fish was higher than that of the cheaper varieties. That's why Magdalen would draw Paklin Bai towards her fish basket with her sharp and loud calling, after having kept the choicest of fish aside, for Paklin Bai to buy. Magdalen was a shrewd seller. She deliberately charged Paklin Bai more than what she would charge other buyers for the same fish. Paklin Bai was aware of this and pretended as though she didn't know.

She still preferred to buy from Magdalen because she observed that Magdalen was smart in presenting the kind of fish that Paklin Bai preferred; for one, it was genuinely fresh and not the one that was stored up in ice and made to appear fresh, secondly, she had sufficient quantities of premium fish, the fat fish as the locals called it. Most importantly Paklin Bai liked the fact that Magdalen made sure she presented the fish in hygienic and neat baskets and would make sure there were no flies anywhere near her fish. Once the buying was done; Magdalen would carefully pack the fish in the netted bag and demonstrate gratitude to Paklin Bai for purchasing from her and would profusely thank her. Then, taking the money from Paklin Bai, she'd throw a quick wink at Claudia as if to say, 'Don't tell your white madam I'm charging her more,' and on her part Claudia chose never to complain to Paklin Bai about Magdalen.

With Bula by her side and the two bags of fish in her hand, now Claudia looked for Magdalen, feeling confident that she could expect Magdalen to help her out. After checking out the prices of the day, she went from one fisherwoman to another to get a good idea of how much the catch of the day was priced at.

Making a mental note about the different pricing, she headed towards Magdalen. Claudia handed the fish bags to Magdalen. Magdalen smiled on seeing the bags full of fish. Being an experienced fisherwoman, it wasn't hard for her to know that the fish was fresh. Much of it was 'fat fish'. Fat fish was bigger in size, better in taste and nutrition and costly in pricing. Claudia had already calculated an estimate of how much money she should receive for the entire lot and mentioned the amount as she released the bags, knowing as a vendor Magdalen could easily fetch double the price on reselling. Magdalen looked at her with eyes opened wide, as though shocked at the price that Claudia suggested. She slid her hand inside her cloth pouch and thrust a handful of cupronickel coins into Claudia's hands with a wily little smile.

'Give it back, Magdalen,' Claudia commanded firmly, after quickly counting the last of the fifteen coins, with an irritated voice. Experience had taught her how to deal with these folk.

Magdalen forced herself to laugh artificially, out of embarrassment and nervousness and quickly pulled out seven more coins and pushed them into Claudia's hand. 'Five more,' Claudia demanded with a sternness that surprised herself.

'Baby, two more is just good enough.'

'Alright. Here's the deal, let's close it at twenty five escudos. Take it or leave it,' Claudia demanded, and Magdalen gave in. Claudia took the money, wrapped half of it in her handkerchief and the other half in the handkerchief she borrowed from Bula. Carefully holding both tight in her hands, she left the bazaar along with Bula.

'Very cleverly done. But don't you forget, you broke my first condition and I'm definitely not going to let you get away with the second,' Bula squealed as they rushed out of the bazaar.

'Condition? What are you talking about Bula?' Claudia exclaimed in surprise.

'Just stop and give me my share,' Bula beseeched as she firmly gripped Claudia's arm and stopped their brisk walk.

'Look Bula, Father needs this money urgently. Let's just run and get home as soon as possible first.'

'Why? To buy himself two more quarters of feni than usual,' Bula thundered with an arrogant stare that contorted her face and made her look almost ugly.

'Bula I told you not to talk like that about Father, here take this. Now run,' Claudia said placing two coins in Bula's hands. Bula refused to run, stopping instead to go to the cola seller. Claudia on the other hand, held the handkerchiefs filled with twenty three escudos closer to her chest, smiling wide within. The metallic clanging seemed to ring like the sound of a fortune into her ears, the sound from the little abundance of coins she had just created out of almost nothing. Claudia was showing early signs of turning her back on the impoverishment that had tried to overrun her family. It took courage to deride the age old blind beliefs of black cats and to devise a false story in exchange for a good portion of fish. It took grit and willpower to have rather than not to have. Proud and happy, she ran homewards.

When she reached home, she saw Father sitting on his favourite wooden stool, still wearing his formal clothes, browsing through an old newspaper. When Claudia offered him the money, he glanced up suddenly, stunned to see the money in her hands. 'Did you go to Gormai?' He asked with a shameful, guilty look, unable to look straight into Claudia's eyes. Claudia held out the money to him in silence, not wanting to reveal how the money came. She could never lie to Father. With a grateful look in his eyes, Father took the money from her hands. He could see her panting from having run and a pang of hurt arose inside his chest. He patted her head, touched her cheek and stretched his thin, shrivelled hand around her shoulder. It was his way of saying Thank you. At that moment, Claudia felt all the missing affection over the years come back in those few seconds of fondness from Father. 'Busha, get a glass of water for Claudia,' Father instructed, as he moved out of the house in a hurry.

Sunday mass

It was quiet when Claudia entered the church. Sunday mass was a crucial part of the weekend in Oroshim; the other important part was lunch with green beef curry along with vinegar salad and rice pulao, yellowed with turmeric; a standard Sunday menu in most Catholic homes. Many locals, the well off and the poor, attended the Portuguese mass; even those who did not understand enough Portuguese came, because it was the first mass of the day.

A compound wall painted in pure white, fenced and fortified the church and the cemetery, freshly bloomed flowers in pink and purple falling across the white walls. Clean walls, green grass, red roses and nodding violets; the church made a bright and beautiful picture on the outside. Claudia often wondered if everything inside was as impeccable; particularly the people, their thinking and things like that.

Claudia's morning look was typical; a clean washed dress, powdered face and a black lace head scarf. She entered the church, looking around, the way she had been doing for most Sundays now. Damiáno had been out of town, on work. She was told that he held a good position in the Portuguese government, and that his work demanded frequent travels to Daman. Claudia was not sure if he would be at church. One thing, if he was back from Daman, he would not miss coming to church.

Two evenings back, at the big house, Claudia had waited eagerly for Paklin Bai to say something about Damiáno, to pick up little clues if she could, from her, to know if he would be back, but she couldn't. She still had a strange feeling that he was coming; Paklin Bai was making pork sausages, a delicacy she took time to prepare only on special occasions. Claudia remembered her telling Mother that Damiáno loves pork sausages. 'Why pork sausages, Paklin Bai, what is so special today?' Claudia wanted to ask, just to know if she was making it specially for Damiáno. She wouldn't know how Paklin Bai would react to her question. Being an open minded, free spirited person, she would often correct her mistakes and teach her the proper way of doing things. She was always polite and respectful. 'Oh Claudia, one must never wait for a reason to celebrate and to relish something they love to eat and drink. *A vida e o amor que criamos sao a vida e o amor que vivemos,* the life and love we create is the life and love we live,' she would say to Claudia cheerfully.

The pinkish white meat, sprinkled with sea salt was diced and placed in a clean straw basket. A heavy grinding stone was placed over it to press out all the water in the pork. Dark, long and dried red chillies, rich cumin, sweet smelling cinnamon, dark cloves, peppercorn, powdered turmeric, cleaned pieces of ginger and cloves of white garlic; the marinade of all the above ingredients was brought to a smooth consistency as Mother took it all through the last few rounds with the grinding stone.

Skilfully and patiently, Paklin Bai mixed the marinade with the meat using her well washed clean soft hands. Claudia stared curiously at the way she was mixing and a feeling of awe arose as the sharp tangy odour of the spices mixed with the meat wafted up her nose. She was all the more tempted to ask if Damiáno would be back by the weekend.

On Sunday, just as she entered the gate of the crowded church, she felt something being slipped into her hand. Without daring to look back, she knew instinctively that it couldn't be anyone else but Damiáno. That moment of surprise caught her off guard and the piece of folded paper he tried slipping into her hand dropped out of her hand. Without any conscious effort, she found herself stopping right there wondering what to do. 'Good day Claudia' she heard a voice from behind and recognised it to be Sankistao who greeted from behind, as she reached the main door at the church entrance. She would have picked up the paper but Sankistao's sudden greeting and the fear of being seen taking the chit from Damiáno, made her nervous.

Tensely, she walked straight inside the church. Seated right across the fourth row, she saw Paklin Bai sitting beside Oliveira Bab and Damiáno. Reverently, Claudia covered her head with her scarf as she moved into one of the available pews and knelt down to pray, as she always did on entering the church. At that moment, she felt an uncontrollable smile lighting up her face. No one smiled or spoke during church service. People were expected to control a smile. And a laugh was the last thing you could think of. You were expected to be still with as little movement as possible and control even a cough or a sneeze.

The paper chit, although inherent with risk, was their only means of communication when they were in public. Damiáno used this means to convey a message to Claudia either at church or at the mansion.

'The grace of our Lord Jesus Christ,
the love of God the Father,
and the communion of the Holy Spirit
be with you all.'

'You may be seated,' uttered the priest, into the microphone, and the congregation reverently obeyed and took their seat. This was the only time you could hear a sound reverberate all through the church as the gathering settled down to their seats. After the ceremonial Sunday rituals, the priest began to deliver the sermon. Claudia's eyes were drawn to the harmoniously decorated glass murals and the intricately sculpted cherubim; some white, some in multi-coloured shades. The high ceiling was designed as a replica of heaven; Angels, clouds, rainbow, stars ... flying doves in plaster-of-Paris, all skilfully crafted. Candle wicks were painted in rich golden yellow. As she stared in awe at the artwork, she wondered if she could talk to the angels and ask them what would be the right and wrong thing to do, ask them what lay ahead for her in life. She tried to listen to the sermon but her eyes seemed to be drawn to the meticulously sculpted heaven in church. Will Damiáno marry me or...? She aborted the question for the angels that arose in her mind and pushed it to a corner of her heart, the corner that suddenly filled with fear, her mind tense because of the little note she had left outside the church door.

At that moment the priest invited the congregation to partake in the penitential act. It was a ritual where each person got an opportunity to confess any sin committed during the past week and ask for forgiveness in order to be in the right spiritual condition to participate in the mass.

'I confess to Almighty God and to you, my brothers and sisters, that I have greatly sinned, in my thoughts and in my words.'

Claudia stopped midway. She couldn't go on with the entire recitation, the words seemed to come alive in her ears as if they were calling out to her for attention. Sin. Sinful deeds. Sinful thoughts. The words echoed loudly in her head. There was so much that had happened of late. She opened her eyes and slowly raised her bowed head.

'In what I have done and in what I have failed to do.' The voice of the entire congregation seemed like one powerful chant as they continued to confess out loud.

She should have been more careful with the paper, she thought, and a sudden tremor ran through her spine at the thought of someone finding it. A silent prayer rose inside her heart, a fervent hope, a plea that no one should be able to get their hands on her chit. The little piece of paper that she longed so much to get from him.

It was time for Holy Communion. At the priest's invitation, people began to move out of their pews in order and walked towards the altar through the aisle. Claudia stood there as the tremors came back, numb and unable to move to receive communion. 'The body of Christ,' the priest uttered before placing a piece of white wafer into each person's mouth taking part in the communion, and each person uttered a soft and almost inaudible Amen.

After everyone who came forward for communion was done receiving the bread, the priest continued with the mass, Claudia daydreaming through most of it. The priest then declared 'Mass has now ended, go in peace.' He raised his hands and blessed the congregation.

Then the crowd exited quietly, forming two queues headed towards the large wooden doors, one of which was flung open. At they reached the single narrow door, the two rows merged into one and people stepped out one at a time. It could have been destiny, a chance, a blessing or an intentional effort from one of them which brought Damiáno and Claudia walking side by side, beside each other. As they eased through the aisle slowly their hands brushed together and it was like a surge of current that passed through her body. The uncontrollable smile returned and she gave in to the overwhelming temptation to look at him and smile. Ignoring the crowd of people all around them. Usually they ensured never to acknowledge each other in public. This time he looked at her and smiled back. She looked up at him again, the smile a bit wider. He smiled back, again and as they inched forward she moved closer towards him, their shoulders kissed for a few seconds until the people on his side of the queue moved out faster than the queue she was in. She was still inside the church while he exited.

Right across the exit arch, Claudia noticed Sankistao standing in the open space. She wondered if he had watched the thing going on between her and Damiáno inside the church as she looked around the ground where the little piece of paper had fallen. From the corner of her eye she watched as Sankistao walked up to her and stretched out a clenched hand towards her. Claudia reached out and took what he offered in silence. It was the same piece of paper that had fallen out of her hand accidentally. Claudia didn't ask him what it was, she didn't have to, knowing the type of paper Damiáno always used to scribble about their meeting, in big letters so she didn't have trouble deciphering what he wrote. When her senses came to an alert, her smile disappeared instantly. What was Sankistao up to? Though she observed everything that went on outside; the congregation greeting one another, the priests conversing lovingly with the people, with most church-attenders engaged in the after service fellowship, Claudia seemed lost. A sudden fear had gripped her. She wished she had not got carried away the way she did after seeing Damiáno at church. She really shouldn't have, knowing how the church attending crowd talked of things. They talked of small things about others; new patterns on dresses or the latest fabrics in fashion, who wore shoes, who wore slippers. Who was bold enough to apply lipstick to church. Who attended the first mass. Who didn't. She could easily be the next target of gossip.

At the moment, all eyes were on the senhor leaving the church compound in his box shaped palanquin; the envied transportation of the privileged. One such privileged person was Luis Bakaar, a village elder and landlord of a big stretch of land in Oroshim. His grand exit, slouched over a palanquin; his daily conveyance, made heads turn. It failed to impress Claudia to watch the poor servants of his house struggling to carry the weight of their master on their frail old shoulders. In a moment she shrugged the pity off. She had more serious matters to worry about.

On Sundays, the bunds were deserted as Claudia made her way back home and slowed down her steps to pull out the little piece of crumpled paper. 'Tomorrow. Same place. Before dawn.' Like always, she made the paper disappear. This time by tearing it into little bits and threw those bits in the slushy field water.

Monday morning, after a bowl of morning kanji, she went to the church kitchen. Sankistao was preparing breakfast for the priests; fried eggs and sausages accompanied by hard bread purchased from the bread seller. Claudia put the kettle on the fire to make tea and set the table as per Padkur's instructions. The priests occupied their seats by the breakfast table. 'Sankistao, here, I made extra tea by mistake,' Claudia said, handing a glass of tea to Sankistao, after serving tea to the priests.

'Well, well, Abel, Claudia makes this mistake often, so it seems. Have it Abel, and don't forget to thank Claudia for her mistake,' Padkur teased, staring sideways at Sankistao. Padre Jose, the senior priest, smiled in silence, finished his breakfast and left. Padkur was called downstairs on some work, his half-eaten breakfast still on the table. 'Claudia, Padkur knows you make extra tea so that I can have it. He knows it's not a mistake. Why do you do that?'

'Because you work hard, you do so much of work in the kitchen and at church. Mother says goat milk gives good strength. Have it, it's getting cold.'

'Will you have some?'

'No Sankistao, my stomach is full; I had two bowls of kanji at home.'

'Two bowls. Good. You are a growing girl. I like to see young people eating well. I don't know why, but you remind me of my daughter in Angola.'

'Honestly, Angola, Sankistao? It's still hard for me to believe you have a daughter, you know.'

'Why not?'

'Because you are a Bombay man.'

'Bombay men do have daughters,' he said. She laughed at his silly joke, like she mostly did.

'Is Angola very near to Bombay?'

'I wish it was. I would visit my princess ever so often,' Sankistao sighed.

'Is she nice?'

'Yes. And maybe these nice girls are the ones who make those mistakes,' he said giving Claudia a look that she didn't really like. It gave her the same feeling as yesterday; making her wonder if he was up to anything fishy.

'Oh! So she made a mistake?'

'She fell in love.'

'But you said love happens just like war.'

'Right. For my girl it happened with a Negro.'

'And he wasn't a good man uh?'

'Oh no no, he was a brilliant young man, but you know a man is expected to return to his people someday and so the day came sooner than we were ready for. He took my only child to

Africa. We did not have the money to travel to Angola nor did they think of coming back to Bombay.'

'Did you cry?'

'I do. Her old mother longed to see her before she died. We only received telegrams from her.'

'Is she happy in Angola?'

'I would like to think so. She has four children. At least we haven't stopped writing to each other.'

'One more question. Can I ask..?'

'Of course my dear.'

'Why does a man have to return to his people?'

'It's a way of life, dear. Claudia, you ask me so many questions, which is fine. If I ask you one question will you answer me with all honesty?' Sankistao asked with the same look in his eyes, the look she had begun to detest now. She couldn't look him in the eye, so she nodded and moved to clear one side of the table, sensing that his question was not going to be easy on her.

'Does Bab Damiáno often ask you to meet him in the dark?'

'What? No ... na, only if there is work .... Why do you ask?' She mumbled her answer, continuing with her work nervously.

'Heat up Padkur's tea girl; he will be back anytime soon to finish his breakfast.'

With Sankistao questioning her with suspicion, she had a doubt that he might even complain to Padkur. It was something most of the elderly folk in the village did when they wanted to stop the young folks from doing anything wrong. Sooner or later she had to face it. She decided to face it now. Get clear with him. To get the burden off her chest about what was on his mind. Although she had to gather up all her courage she made bold to ask 'Sankistao, tell me, who gave you that paper, yesterday at church?'

He stared at her, a bit taken aback, and was silent for a moment before answering. 'I saw Bab Damiáno give it to you as you entered church, and it fell off from your hand. I picked it up,' he said, and continuing with a little sigh added, 'I read it before giving it to you after the mass had ended.'

'What if I had hesitated to take it from you?'

'Then I would be in two minds, though I still feel your white master is out to woo you.'

'Sankistao, listen. Whatever you know about this, please keep it to yourself. And he is not out to woo me. He is a decent man. Please don't say anything to anyone,' Claudia pleaded, her face drenched in sweat, her eyes showing a strange fearfulness.

'If I were you, I'd be cautious, Claudia.'

They heard Padkur's steps as he climbed up the staircase.

'Please Sankistao ...' she pleaded again, this time with folded hands, in a whisper. He nodded absentmindedly, giving her a long, baffled look.

Sipping his tea, Padkur spoke. 'Abel, I am running late. Socorrina will come for her baptismal certificate; it is ready on the office table. The catechism children will start today. They will come by afternoon, spread a mat for them. Claudia don't forget to fill the pots, children will need water for drinking. Abel, clean and refill the baptismal font,' he instructed, finished his breakfast in a hurry and moved.

Banana leaf wrapped sausages

It was late evening when Claudia returned from the fields with Gormai. Something was different at home. Father was sitting sober and dressed in clean clothes. He had that rare look on, the one that came to his face only under special conditions; this was usually when he abstained from alcohol for a day or even a few hours, or if he had fever or was attending someone's funeral or wedding nuptials, or if it was Good Friday. Since it was none of the above events, Claudia tiptoed inside, curious to know what was going on but anxious too.

Mother was pouring out tea carefully in the porcelain mugs; the greatly prized and one of the only remaining wedding gifts Claudia's parents had received. The mugs, apart from the exquisite jewellery box with the dancing ballerina were the only things that Father had not bartered for liquor. The mugs were draped in an old dress and hidden under the clothes in Mother's wooden almirah and were taken out only when guests were at home. It was common within the neighbourhood to have special crockery which was taken out only when there were guests.

Jakin was arranging butter biscuits in a plate, Bula munching bits of them greedily, biscuits not usually available at home. Guests! At our home! Claudia exclaimed in her mind. But who could they be? Relatives and neighbours hardly came to visit them, unless it was some sort of a matchmaking visit. Curious to find, she leaned closer towards the old curtain that separated the kitchen and the sitting place.

The clothing of the visitors was not really familiar to the Goan or Portuguese way of dressing. Some of them wore cloth caps; the language they spoke was strange too. Mother said it was Hindustani. Claudia strained her ears to listen to their talks. They spoke of civil liberties, freedom for Goans that was long overdue, jobs, Bombay, etc. From the sound of it all, it seemed less of a matchmaking talk and more of something pro-war. Anti-Portuguese! Could they be the same Indians, rumoured to soon drive away the Portuguese? Perhaps! Those were the same men that Sankistao had been telling her about. But why would they visit Father? She couldn't wait to find out.

Claudia often asked Sankistao about the political situation, especially after Damiáno Bab told her about censorship laws concerning the press and publishing which she was not fully able to understand. That's when Sankistao explained to her that after India's independence from British Raj, Prime Minister Jawaharlal Nehru began to work on a diplomatic solution to liberate Goa from the Portuguese colonisation. He explained that while Nehru's argument was that the people of Goa were Indians, the Portuguese Prime Minister, António de Oliveira Salazar argued that Goa was a Portuguese province and an integral part of Portugal. Also, he said, according to Salazar, Goans did not consider themselves as Indians but Portuguese and while the debate between them continued, India, motivated by Gandhian philosophies of non violence, pursued the Goa liberation movement, urging Goans to fight for liberation from the Portuguese colonisation. Sankistao also explained how, perhaps not wanting the opposition party publicising stories across Europe that the Portuguese were not treating the Goans well, António de Oliveira Salazar was strict about the censorship laws concerning publishing any material or news, even about holding public meetings.

Could that be the reason this little group of people wanted to meet secretly in her house? Claudia wondered.

'Sorry my dear, you must be Bula. Did I hurt you? I was coming inside to greet your mother.' The man who had walked through like a headless chicken said apologetically. Not looking at what was ahead, he had failed to notice Claudia behind the curtain separating the sitting place and the kitchen. It hurt badly for a moment when the man's head dashed into Claudia's.

'No Santu, that's not Bula, that's Claudia, our youngest one.' Mother corrected the visitor, her tone friendly and calm.

'Busha! How are you, my dear? Been long. More than five years, isn't it?'

'Much more than that, Santu, almost ten. You forgot that we are alive.'

'Oh Busha, if I forgot I wouldn't be here. It is my love that brings me here. Do you have any idea how much I have missed your family and my dear friend, your husband? Come on,' the man said, giving Mother a warm hug.

'Jakin, Bula, Claudia, do you remember Ti Gomes ... Santu Gomes?' Mother had a wide smile that stretched her face and lit up her eyes.

'Father's best friend. Isn't it?' Jakin acknowledged.

'He was,' Mother teased.

'Busha. Busha, there you go again. I am still your father's best friend, girls, don't get misled by your mother. Back in those days, your father and I sparked quite some fireworks in our village.' Gomes chuckled at his own statement.

So this was him, the best friend that moved to Bombay and never bothered visiting Father, even though he visited the village during most summers. Mother, Gormai, Jakin, Bula and some other neighbours had mentioned him often. He is more than a brother, Father would say about him. They both were behind organising tiatr and events in Oroshim, back in those days. Claudia remembered hearing about the man; Santu Gomes.

'Ti, Aren't those men Indians, why are they here?' Claudia questioned, disturbed by the men's presence in her house.

'Dear! They just wanted a place to discuss some issues. I bumped into your father the other day at Matil Mashen's tavern and asked him if I can bring them along. They will leave soon,' Ti Gomes answered, taken aback a bit by Claudia's question.

'Will there be a war?' Claudia asked.

'No. The Nehru government is not in favour of war. It is not an option, unless we are attacked by the opposition. Panditji himself has mentioned that the government thinks Goa has a distinct individuality. The government will preserve our culture, religion, language. Everything. Our Goa will continue to have its independent presence under the Indian Government. Non-violence was Bapuji's success. Look at India now, a free India, a happy India, free from colonialism and oppression. Panditji has been with Bapuji, he knows what's best.'

Claudia didn't understand much of what he said, but she was sure she wouldn't like any men that came to drive the Portuguese away. Coming closer to all of them in the kitchen, Santu Gomes lowered his voice almost to a whisper. 'The situation outside is not favourable for them to meet openly, they needed a secure place. That's all. Nothing to worry. If these men meant any harm, would I bring them close to you all? Never. Your family is my family. You girls were too small to know the special bond that I and your father shared.'

'What have the Portuguese done to them, why are they trying to send them away?' Claudia persisted.

'Sshhh,' Mother tried to stop her.

'Wait Busha, let the child speak. Let them know the truth. What's your name baby?'

'Claudia.'

'Hm. Claudia. Wouldn't you like a good job for Father? These men are trying to make it happen for us, for the Goans, for our Oroshim people. Soon our situation will get better.'

'Haven't the Portuguese already made our situation better? They gave us clothes to wear, food, money, work, so much! All of it comes from Paklin Bai.'

'True! But it's not the food and clothes that will free our people, dear. Freedom is not filling our stomachs only; but to help us stand on our feet to buy our own food and take care of our families.'

'But a full stomach is what we had needed; we would not have enough food in the house, we slept hungry many times, until we started working for Paklin Bai's family. Mother and I are very happy to work there. Aren't we Mother?'

'Of course, dear. I am sure you and Mother are happy to work for Paklin Bai. They are not saying your Paklin Bai is bad. It's not that the Indians hate the Portuguese people. It is about the civil rights, about liberation. The Portuguese are occupying a part of India as if it's a part of them, and that needs to be dealt with. You are still young to understand civil rights, of course, we do not understand it all at this point of time, and that's fine, but there is going to be a great change, in time we all will understand.'

'But they say the Portuguese have already changed us in a good way. Look at Father, once he would wear a loin cloth but now, he wears trousers. Men here, look dignified now than what they'd look in that loin cloth.'

Father joined in while the discussion still went on in the kitchen. He handed Mother the rolled up strings of pork sausages wrapped inside a crumpled newspaper. 'Father, didn't you tell Ti Gomes, how in your boyhood years the Portuguese helped you get rid of the loin cloth and wear trousers instead? Do you remember you told us you dodged the officials on the streets, when they did a check on the loin cloth?'

Santu Gomes' laughter had a sound like that of a soda fizz when a bottle is shaken and the cork abruptly taken off. The funny sound spread all over the kitchen. Then he threw his arm around Father and chuckled even more. 'I didn't think you would spill out our boyhood secrets to your daughters. Dodging the officials? Yes of course. We were together in it. Pants on the roads, but loin cloth on reaching the fields. Oh my good Lord. The Portuguese insisted on not wearing our loin cloth in public, until then we were quite comfortable in our red chequered cloth. We cared less walking long routes; crossing water ponds, climbing hillocks, trying everything possible, just to avoid wearing trousers and not get caught in our favourite little kashti.' Santu Gomes went on. One could tell Father, standing closer to him, with an amused happy face longed to say something, opening his mouth but stopping himself, finally he gave in and added, 'The fishermen and the toddy tappers are lucky, the cloth still covers them even when they are up the tree.'

'Covers them or still uncovers them?' Santu remarked, and they laughed more. It was strange to watch Father talk and laugh so much. And as though his laughter had touched Mother's lips, Mother laughed too. For long, a laughter like that had not been heard in the house. Suddenly, everyone seemed to have forgotten that Claudia was annoyed, so she too decided to let go, joining in the laughter, especially when she saw Jakin and Bula giggling.

The Indian men, done with their discussion, spoke a while to Santu, thanked Father and left. Later, Santu Gomes and Father sat for a drink. It took them past midnight to finish the bottle that Gomes had brought. Mother, Bula and Jakin slept. Claudia lay pretending to be asleep; wanting to stay awake to hear the conversation. Refill after refill from the tall feni bottle, and the tin mugs tinkled as the bottle touched the mug rims. Father spoke of good things; about Jakin and Bula and about Mother. And they thought Father didn't have anything favourable to say about them. Father was revealing his good side, the one that he displayed in his youthful days, the kind that the three girls didn't really have the luck to witness in recent years. The way he was carrying himself in Santu's presence surprised Claudia. She suddenly heard the name 'Claudia' mentioned. She strained her ears more in order to hear every word.

'You have an extraordinary girl there.'

'Santu, Santu, you have hardly heard her. She talks fantastic. You must come and listen to her sometimes.'

'Has any boy's family asked for her?' Santu asked inquisitively.

'O! The girl has a queue lined up to ask for her hand,' Father replied. Now he is bragging, trying to show off with Santu, Claudia said in her mind. Claudia didn't think he was aware of the pack of cards that had been lying unused among the old dusty books, but it seemed like Father remembered where the cards were. After a few games the pitch in their voices raised, accompanied by more frequent bouts of laughter as the feni began to kick in getting them more drunk. Santu Gomes won two games, Father won three; Father leading in the game. It thrilled Claudia, she felt proud of Father.

Mother had prepared pork sausages wrapped in a big banana leaf, grilling them slowly over burning coal. Father and his friend relished it along with the drinks. Father got to a bragging again; he told Gomes he should come and taste the way Mother makes the country fowl xacuti. After a while Santu Gomes rose to his feet, hugging Father goodbye, slipping a roll of money into Father's hands before leaving the house. That day, there was something more precious than money that he left behind; a smile on Father's face. A good man had guests in his house, at least, that's how the villagers judged a person's character and social status. That's how the neighbours showed off by inviting many guests. Father closed the doors and pushed the wooden bolt of the front door into its slot. He whistled with a loud melodious tune, oblivious to the disturbance it might cause to those asleep in the house. Santu Gomes' intention to visit Father could have been anything; good, not good, commercial, whatever it was, Claudia was elated to know that somebody was able to put a smile on her father's face. Strange though, that all it took to lift one man's discouraged spirit was the company of another man, that's all. It was something Father had missed. For too long he was ridiculed, discriminated, rejected, when he had loved his friends so much. Like the house lamp that flickers when it runs out of oil but soon the flames reignite when a little oil is added to its emptiness, so was Father with his emptiness, and Santo Gomes was the little drop of oil.

Claudia liked him. Felt grateful that there was someone who had the ability to make Father laugh and whistle loudly once again.

Piedade Ferrao to marry Claudia

'I can't see you tomorrow, Bab.' Claudia said, sitting cross-legged on top of the brick walls of the ruins. Damiáno was stretched out with his head resting on her lap. The fingers of her right hand were clasped tight into his left hand and with his other hand he stroked her hair and face.

'What have I done now?' Damiáno asked, mischief in his tone.

At other times that question would have amused Claudia, not today. Her mind was filled with serious thoughts. 'Mother and I must collect dung at dawn for the big cooking shed. Paklin Bai wants the mansion to be done up before Christmas arrives,' she told him.

'So the cooking shed gets more attention than me.'

'You know that's not true Bab. How can anything be more important than you?'

'I was only teasing. What's wrong minha querida? Something seems to be troubling you.'

'Just thinking Bab.'

'Thinking? What thinking my dear?' Damiáno asked, his fingers reaching below her neck with soft strokes. Her light yellow taffeta dress had big red buttons on the front and a red zigzag lace bordering along the collar. It also had two little pockets to tuck little things like tamarind seeds or roasted grams which she often nibbled on.

'Bab,' she said, letting out a little moan as his hands wandered over her.

Their meetings always began with casual talk. Once the ice was broken with silly chatter, they would take time to do things they both enjoyed with each other. Moments of intimacy and pleasure that often left both of them breathless yet wanting more. Their meetings were also times of learning for Claudia. Often, Damiáno would correct her grammatical errors; the ruins would then turn into a Portuguese class. He had a great sense of humour and would often say something funny to make her giggle. He loved to watch her laugh freely, unreservedly, at his jokes. It always charmed his heart and drew them closer, more intimately to each other. These were special offerings they had for each other. His subtle, yet innocent, harmless humour, his calm confidence, the sensitivity he displayed to understand where to draw the line, his self control and the power of his hands that soothed her body with every touch. In exchange, she offered him a quiet innocence that allowed him a sense of freedom with her. She was bold to come and meet him at a time of the day that not many girls would dare to step out into the bushes. She drew out his affection in ways that brought him much pleasure. Clean, pure, sensuous. And the softness of her skin always made him yearn to touch her more and the pure affection she offered in return caused him to come back to her for more.

'What's on your mind, dear?'

'Bab, I am wondering how it will be when you and I are married and gone our own ways.' Claudia said, wondering how to break the harsh news to him. 'The Ferrao's son, who works on a ship, wants to get married to me this New Year. Gormai has given his family a word for me,' she announced, her voice grave.

'What? Who? What is his name?'

'Piedade Ferrao. We have to stop meeting like this Bab.'

'Claudia, have you said yes to the wedding?'

'Yes Bab. I had to. It means a lot to my family, it will be the biggest excitement for Father especially, he doesn't know about it yet, but when he does get to know about it, trust me Bab, it will be the greatest news of his life.'

'Do you like the boy?'

'I have not seen him yet. It seems he and I used to play together as children. He would spend summer in Oroshim at Gormai's brother's house. He is related to them. And our family would accompany Gormai to their house during summer holidays. I was too small then, I don't remember him, but it seems he does; obviously, he was much older than me.'

'So he never forgot you since then?'

'Maybe.' She responded with shyness. 'Will you be happy for me Bab?'

He looked into her eyes, cupped her face fondly in his warm hands and answered, 'Who wouldn't be happy for anything good that happens to you Claudia. Come here.' He pulled her closer, whispering in her ears the sweet names that she loved to hear from him. 'You are a beautiful girl, minha querida, and the man who is with you will always be a happy man.'

'Paklin Bai talks about the Portuguese girls she is looking for you, is it true? If yes, then it's time for us to stop meeting like this. It's really bad if someone finds us meeting like this Bab, don't you think so?'

'Never thought of that, Claudia. Is that what you want us to do? Cover your head. The dew can give you a cold' he said, passing on his handkerchief.

She cuddled closer to his broad chest. For a few moments he was quiet, pondering over what Claudia said. After a prolonged silence, he suddenly asked, 'Are you afraid, Claudia?'

With the winter season about to set in, the farmers had begun sleeping at night in the field, most of them watering their crops as early as four in the morning. The bunds were no longer as deserted as in the monsoon. The Oroshim villagers were brave and hard working; whether it was the harsh chill of the winter or the humidity of the summer, the farmers worked laboriously in the fields. It was only during heavy rains, lightning and harsh winds, some of them were left without much option but to stay away, temporarily from the fields, usually around the month of August, on days when the wind was harsh and rains extremely excessive. Then, as the severity of the rainy days subsided, they resumed work, back to labouring again. Except in the rainy season, many of the farmers stayed in the field itself, in a little thatched hut they built, especially to sleep at night. In winters, they warmed themselves through a bonfire made of dried weed and sticks and in summer they kept themselves cool by bathing in the cold field pond water.

Claudia and Damiáno had created their own little love corner in the middle of the bushes, a bit distant from the fields. They too began to meet much early, around 3:00 am to enjoy their intimate privacy. They made sure to meet at least once a week, if Damiáno was not away in Daman. At home, they were under an impression that she was out to collect the early morning fall of dry coconuts, palm leaves, fruits or flowers; hence Claudia had the freedom to step out of the house early in the morning, and though she did pick up some of those coconuts and things, she also took advantage of the freedom she was allowed.

Claudia often imagined how it would be if the trees around them could talk, after all they seemed to see and hear everything that went on between her and her Damiáno Bab. As she looked around, she felt deeply grateful to the natural surroundings all around for favouring their togetherness; the calm shade of the huge gum tree provided a roof above them, wild creepers and thick bushes made walls to hide them from every eye around Baretto's old house, the early morning darkness gave them unrestrained freedom. Freedom that the brightness of day denied. The hay in the stack was their warm bed during the chilly, deserted hours, the broken brick walls, rocks or mud bunds their seating arrangement. Dry shrubs and weeds fuelled the bonfire to keep them warm on extremely cold mornings.

'I am a little afraid Bab,' Claudia confessed.

'Then why are you...?'

'Getting married...?'

'Hm. Well, not that...' he shook his head, reluctantly.

'I must Bab, else my family will not have a place in Oroshim, and the elders will send us away. I am doing this for Father. All these years, nothing good worked out for him although he tried much.'

'Nothing good worked for him?'

'Father once had a decent job at a printing press which closed down; it left him without any income for too long. It was then that a rich man in Bombay offered him an assignment. Very reluctantly, Father took it up and picked up the dangerous trade fast. The fat, rich boss was pretty impressed with Father. We would have been richer than Luis Bakaar, if he had continued with him. Those days we had begun to eat like the Bakaars; soup, beef curry, pulao, all at the table. Father had even bought a bicycle.'

'Why was the trade dangerous?'

'Because he carried the contraband.'

'What? Contraband...?' he asked her, stunned at her words.

'So you don't know what is contraband. You see Bab, at that time I would ask Father a lot of questions about what the contraband was. Father used to explain to me everything, making it easy on me to be discreet and silent and prepared. "Claudia, we Goans use lot of gold; women as well as men, besides we make gold idols, and wear gold crosses and sculpted religious lockets around the chains. So a lot of gold is shipped into Goa from places like Mozambique, Macau and the Persian gulf. Some of that gold is smuggled to places in India, through illicit ways,' Father would explain. But not just gold Bab, other precious commodities like watches and diamonds were a part of it too. We would travel to places like Bombay and Karwar, I can't recollect names of other places but those days I travelled much with Father and his smuggling companions.'

'I know what contraband means dear, but I was a bit taken aback to hear it from you. What did the fat boss ask you to do for him, Claudia?'

'Nothing Bab. I was a child then, and having a child along had its own perks. Father took me along so that nobody was suspicious about what he did. Soon we learnt the tricks to dodge the police when they raided the lodges looking for gold smugglers. Often, we walked long distances searching for small lodges away from the city to avoid suspicion. We had the police knocking on our door many times, but Father escaped because of me being around.

'We always travelled in groups, never alone. We never knew who would be part of the group or how large the group would be. We always shared the room with each other, pretending to be a family that stayed together. We would conceal the contraband carefully in parts of our body and camouflage it with multiple layers of clothing. What a lovely ethnic Indian skirt they had got for me; It had multi-colour mirror work on its borders, embroidered with many elephants. Most of the time, we would be either travelling on a train or a large steamer. As with other things, we would not be told about the mode of travel in advance.'

'I must say you are very courageous Claudia,' Damiáno interrupted with an impressed look in his eyes.

‘Yes, most of the time, Bab. Yet, there were times when we all would be afraid. Once, we almost got caught. I remember walking through narrow lanes late in the evening to find the lodging. Once I reached it and went into the damp and dusty room, I smiled on seeing a mat spread below the wooden cot. I was relieved that I had the opportunity to sleep. The feeling of lying on my back and stretching my aching legs after sitting in a cramped train the whole day was wonderful. With the tiredness, it wasn’t difficult to fall asleep in spite of the surroundings.

I’m not sure how long I slept but I was suddenly woken up by a woman who shared the lodging with us. She roughly began to shake me out of my sleep. She shushed me with her hand on my mouth and dragged me to the bathing area, briskly removed my blouse and skirt and overturned the full bucket of water over my head and body. It was winter and the water was icy cold. My body shuddered as I shivered, drenched in the wetness.

She whispered with a fearful look and said the police had raided the lodge and were checking everyone. Some of the others sharing the room with us tried to hide under the cot. Father lay on the cot. One woman rushed to the bathing area and pretended to bathe. The woman who poured water over me told me to open the door. I hesitated because I was wearing just my cotton petticoat and I was drenched wet but I knew the situation was sensitive and when Father signalled to me to obey the woman, I slowly opened the door. By then the banging on the door had increased in intensity. The moment I opened the door, three policemen in khakis stood outside with a serious expression. “Where are your parents?” they questioned.

'Mother and I were having a bath,' I blurted out, saying the first thing that came to my mind. The men spoke to each other and laughed among themselves.

'The serious look they had on disappeared and they turned and walked away. I wondered what they must have said that seemed to amuse them so much. The moment they left, I quickly shut the door and bolted it from inside. I couldn't sleep after that. The slightest noise made me alert, thinking the policemen might return. They never returned.

'Father had to be extremely alert in this smuggling thing, apart from being honest and faithful to his wealthy boss. Workers cheating the man would face harsh consequences: lashing and more. But not Father, he had earned the trust and favour of his boss. Unfortunately bad news awaited us on one of our return trips to Oroshim. The news shocked Father.'

'News?'

'The news about Jakin doing wrong things. She fell in love with a man who was already married, so I am told Bab. You know our Oroshim elders are very strict about things that are moral and upright, especially with the unmarried girls. Father's trouble didn't end with Jakin. Later, Bula was caught doing something similar. Mother convinced Father to leave everything and stay at home. Those days he would do anything that Mother asked him to. He took up a job at a new printing press, he was happy to do it, despite not making as much money in that job as he did in smuggling. Soon the new press closed down. It was after so many things failed him in life, that he began spending more time at the taverns; drinking on credit.'

'Minha querida, in all the time we spent together, I never asked you about your family. I can help your Father find a job again.'

'Bab, he tried. Just a few days back he got a new job, he went for a day or two, they warned him not to drink on duty, but he did. He didn't tell us but he told one of the workers there that he gets body tremors if he stops drinking.'

'Oh dear, don't be sad. You are a brave girl, Claudia. It will be well. I get this feeling, that you and your family will be fine.'

'What about you Bab. How much time until you marry?'

'Minha querida, please, let's talk of something else.'

'It's alright Bab, the sun will be out soon.'

'Right dear. Everything has its time in life Claudia, the dawn, the dusk, the struggles, the joys, the sun too. Can a man try to contend with time and season?'

'Is that written in the book?'

'Book?'

'As in, those beautiful things you say at times, I like them Bab. Do you learn that in the books you read?'

'No, you don't always learn everything from books, dear.'

'No? Then you are very intelligent Bab, yet so simple and warm. I will never forget you.'

'Until a man arrives from the ship?....' he teased.

'I swear on my life Bab, this heart's special place will belong to you and none else.' Claudia said as she pressed his hand tightly against her chest, on her heart, as if she was sealing the words with a promise. 'It's my promise, Bab...'

'Oh my dear Claudia ...' he tried to say something but Claudia interrupted.

'Bab, the sun is coming up. It's time to go.' She tried getting up slowly as he held her down tightly, not letting her get up. She looked at him in surprise. Wondering what he wanted. 'Is it already time to go minha querida?' He asked with a disappointed tone as he drew close to her face and kissed her ears, his hand clutching her face.

'Yes Bab,' she whispered back.

'Dear, you will be fine. Life is a teacher, you will learn much from that teacher.' He laughed softly without even meaning to laugh. He was trying to hide his real emotions.

Bula desires Damiáno

Claudia walked faster, the cold morning air blowing against her.

'The rabbit hides its eyes and thinks no one saw it.' The sudden familiar voice from behind alarmed her. She was trying to get back home after the early morning tryst with her lover. Hearing the voice, she slowed down in nervousness. Face it or just run, she wondered which one to choose, with a quick glance to look back impulsively. 'I knew it was you Bula. Why are you following me?' She questioned angrily. Bula came from behind and stood in front, blocking her way. 'You clever fox. You can't get away with this,' she said to Claudia with a jealous tone.

'Let me go, Bula. What do you want?'

'That depends on what you can give me.'

'My peach and white dress and all the coins I saved up in the tin. Now let me go. Please.' Claudia pleaded trying to dodge Bula and move forward.

'Oh Claudia, your front button is open, did you forget or did you unbutton yourself for him?'

'Shut up your mouth, Bula.'

'Don't you tell me to shut up, you cunning thing. So naive and innocent before people and when they are asleep? Tell me, who should I go to first. Father. Gormai. Padkur. You'll be finished,' Bula blurted and grabbed Claudia's hair tightly.

'Leave my hair, Bula. It hurts.'

'It won't hurt if you stop thinking of Damiáno Bab. From today, I will go to the mansion to work with Mother. You are going to tell Mother your leg is hurt badly.'

'You Thief! Why do you always want whatever I have?'

'Let's bandage that leg of yours and tell Mother you can't go to work, unless you want me to go to Gormai and tell her you were in the bushes with ...'

'Enough. Fine. I'll do it.'

'Bandage the leg?'

'Yes.'

'Tell Mother you are unable to go to work?'

'Yes.'

'And you will stop meeting him from today.'

'Good Lord. Why are you so difficult, Bula?'

They continued to argue on their way back home. Bula stuck to her threat. Jakin had still not woken up, Father too. In the quietness, Bula managed to get one of Father's old note books to pull a blank page out of it, the paper crackled as she tore it. She then found a pencil and held the paper and pencil out to Claudia.

'What should I write?'

'My dear Damiáno. Meet me at the same place tomorrow at the same time, your loving, Claudia.'

'Bula Please. You don't even know what you are doing.'

'Just write the note or ...'

Bula was a difficult person to handle. Selfish, stubborn and unpredictable. Claudia knew that she could do anything to have her way. She had to be sensitive about the way she handled Bula, now that she knew about her and Damiáno. Claudia wrote the note. She bandaged her leg with a piece of cloth. When it was time to leave, she showed her leg to Mother and said it was hurting too bad and she would not be able to go to the mansion with her today.

Bula volunteered and Mother took her along to the big house while Claudia remained at home, anxious about what was going to happen. Deep inside, she hoped Damiáno would not believe Bula, ever. Unable to sit at home with the anxiety getting too much, she decided to walk up to Gormai's house. Plucking one of the ripe guavas from the tree in Gormai's frontyard, she started eating it and saw Gormai in the backyard, cleaning fish.

Claudia offered to help. 'Be careful, the korbot has fine bones, this small fish,' said Gormai and moved a bowl of fish towards Claudia. 'The more difficult in cleaning, the tastier the curry,' Gormai chuckled with a wise look in her eyes.

'I think korbot curry is the tastiest of all curries. Isn't it Gormai? I wish I knew how to make it the way Jakin makes it.'

'If Jakin can make it why can't you, it is not a hard task,' Gormai said, not really interested in hearing anything good about Bula or Jakin. Gormai, with her interest in matchmaking and seeing the young girls and boys in the village settled well in marriage, seemed to have not forgiven Jakin and Bula for their bad conduct.

Gormai began telling Claudia the easiest way to make the fish curry with korbot. 'First, just grind the usual fish curry masala all together into a paste, give it a good boil and then add kokum. To make it more pungent, add a few pounded teppal seeds. Add finely cut onion and chopped tomatoes, a couple of green chillies slit into two.'

'Cutting onion is the part that I hate. My eyes start watering and they burn like anything.'

'Once you get used to cooking, you will get used to it Claudia. We all did.'

'I will try, Gormai.'

'Try? Not enough my girl. A woman should master her own unique cooking skill; don't you know, the way to a man's heart is through his stomach? It's one sure way to keep her man indoors. Besides, a woman must learn to read, that way you can read the holy book of litany, and letters received from loved ones overseas. A woman who knows how to read will always find respect. And I must tell you Claudia, the girl who takes time to embroider a table cloth or two and learn the art of stitching out a few pillow cases, will always keep her husband's home beautiful. What happened to your leg girl; let me see, is it a bad fall?' Gormai concluded the lecture on the best attributes for a woman she had learnt over the years.

'Just a small cut. I am fine Gormai. Though, I don't understand why a girl has to go all the way to someone else's home and decorate it too.'

'Her husband's home is the place where she belongs. It's where a woman looks more beautiful.'

'O Gormai! I thought we were talking about korbot curry,' Claudia said, hoping to change the topic which seemed to make her a bit uncomfortable. Give my old woman something to pick on and there's no end to her preaching, Claudia grumbled in her mind. 'Ah yes. So where were we with the korbot curry recipe?' Gormai asked, her mind simultaneously engaged in her cooking.

'Chopping onions and cutting tomatoes ...' Claudia exclaimed jokingly.

'Correct. Add it all to the boiling masala. Stir for five minutes and as the water gets thicker add the juice of tamarind soaked for at least an hour, that way the tamarinds release their best juice. Meanwhile, make sure you clean the korbot fish well.'

'Delicious!' exclaimed Claudia pretending to lick her lips.

'You got your grandfather's taste buds, girl. May his soul rest in peace.' Gormai uttered a quick prayer.

'Grandfather liked korbot curry?'

'You bet he did. You were not even born then. He would go fishing obsessed with the hope of catching some korbot. He didn't fancy even fat fish but relished his korbot curry. He called it a poor man's rich feast. My old man licked his fingers and the plate every time I made korbot curry at home,' Gormai narrated fondly, letting out a shy laugh, like a young maiden talking of her first love.

'Gormai, you always go pink with happiness each time you talk of Grandfather. I heard he had a good sense of humour and made you laugh a lot.'

'He was a good man. He did drink and all, but he was a man who knew his limits. Occasionally we both enjoyed a few shots of feni together, but never got addicted to that stuff. You know Claudia, things were not always easy during my days too, and there wasn't laughter all the time. Your grandfather had his own weaknesses which were quite a challenge to deal with. But I learnt to deal with issues through patience. I'm telling you my dear, patience is a woman's greatest virtue. A wise wife will always bring strength to a weak husband. That way the marriage grows stronger and lasts longer.' Gormai wiped her wrinkled brow.

'Did it take you long to like him after your wedding day?'

'I liked him way before my wedding day. From the very first moment my eyes caught a glimpse of him, truth be told,' Gormai said, lowering her voice to a milder, secret-telling volume.

'Love marriage oh! How wonderful! Tell me more.'

'Oh girl, I don't know what that means but we had a marriage and I loved him from the moment I saw him. Let me tell you our story. One day, when I was about your age, I was working in the fields. It was harvest time. I cannot ever forget that afternoon. It was the day the good lord above caused the sun to light up the skies above the fields to bless me with a sight I never expected. I saw, right in front of me, a man with a countenance like no man I had ever seen. Handsome and ruddy in appearance. Well built. Tall and strong looking. He moved with the confidence of a lion as the magnificence of the first sun rays shone directly over him. He seemed to gallop through the fields and over the hills with the might of a horse; flaunting his

God-given charm and I could not take my eyes off him, until he passed my field.' Gormai continued, a girlish look appearing on her face.

'And then?'

'The next thing I knew was that I was kneeling in the field, right there in the muck. With folded hands I was staring into the heavens with a prayer on my lips that came from the deepest part of my being. Please Almighty God, send me that man. Please send his parents to ask my parents for my hand in marriage.'

'Oh Gormai, that is so romantic.'

'Wait till you hear the rest of it. I am not done yet, my girl. The days that went by had my mind filled with that first sight. I replayed that memory over and over in my mind. I just could not stop myself from thinking of that strikingly handsome man and his confident running through our field. A few days later I was told that there was someone coming to see me. That day I wore a white petticoat with a lace border which I had stitched myself. And was I glad that I did wear it, because as I stood in the field, I got a glimpse of the sight again. It was the same vigour-filled man at our fields. The good Lord granted me my miracle. I wanted to make sure I flaunted the white lace of my new petticoat, not wasting any time in tucking up the cotton long skirt a little higher. No girl was supposed to make a conversation with a man coming to ask her hand. Most girls were shy, though I could not wait to get his attention.'

'So you?'

'I asked him a question.'

‘What question?’

‘I asked what time he usually passes by our fields, and he promptly replied to me saying he will pass by the next day as soon as the sun is out.’

‘And then he met you every day and both of you spoke about marriage. He said yes and you said yes.’

‘It didn’t work that way in those days for us. Our parents had to say yes which they had to with the good Lord on my side. No regrets. He was indeed a good man. How I wish he was around, you would enjoy spending time with your grandfather. It’s very windy today, isn’t it, girl? Winter is breaking. If it was sunny, I would dry some of this fish,’ Gormai said, looking up at the clear sky.

‘Gormai, do you think the Almighty will send a miracle husband to every girl if they ask?’

‘Most certainly! And I pray that the Almighty will send you the right man, Claudia. My heart says something good is coming your way soon. May you make the most wonderful wife and mother. I pray that you will meet the right man and find the right house.’ Gormai cupped Claudia’s face in her hands and kissed her forehead with a blessing.

‘Now that lunch is done let me take a look at your leg. I can put some vinegar on it.’

‘Oh no Gormai. Vinegar burns bad.’

‘Yes and it speeds up the healing. Come on now, don’t want you going around with a cut for too long.’

‘Don’t worry Gormai. I am fine. I must go now.’ Claudia said and rose up to rush home.

Back home, the war with Bula was still strong on Claudia's mind. It got harder when she tried imagining Bula handing Damiáno the note and to think of Bula spending time with him. Along with the painful speculation, a thought of consolation ran through her mind. She suddenly remembered Damiáno had mentioned to her, that he might be leaving that afternoon for Daman. Claudia immediately clasped her hands and a silent prayer escaped her lips. 'Please Almighty Lord. Let the vehicle that takes Damiáno to Daman come,' she whispered with all the hope she could muster. It was the first time she wished he would go away.

The painful wait for Mother and Bula to return began.

One look at Bula's face and Claudia could tell what must have happened. She knew all about Bula's expressions. Jumping up and down and grinning with a silly smile when happy and grumpy and silent when something goes wrong. Jakin was sitting on the wooden stool having lunch, a second time. It was how the girls ate; whenever there was tasty fish curry the girls ate their lunch twice, sometimes thrice. Most people in the village did that. Bula returned, back home earlier than expected. As Jakin rose to wash her plate, Bula came closer to Claudia, and stared at her with an angry look on her face. 'Listen. It seems he is gone to Daman. But he is not gone forever. You go there right now and help Mother, I am tired. That Paklin Bai has too much work there. Mother is doing it alone,' she shot with irritation in her voice.

'Tired already?' Claudia asked sarcastically looking back at Bula with a smile that said, 'I won.'

'You don't talk too much. Just go.' Bula retorted, pulling at Claudia's hair.

'Leave my hair alone, Bula,' Claudia squealed, rising up from her seat. The joy of knowing Damiáno had left numbed the pain caused by Bula. With a skip in her step, she hurried to the mansion. The weather was just getting pleasant, thanks to the onset of winter. Claudia felt like she could swirl her skirt around, dance on the bunds, sing out a song, shout on top of her voice, Hurrah! Damiáno was gone. Bula couldn't get him after all. The Almighty Lord does answer heartfelt prayers she thought as a silent thanks rose in her heart.

And as she raised her head towards the skies, she watched the great big eagles soaring high. The wind blew hard across the field, carrying large quantities of dry leaves from the tall trees, scattering them far and wide. The cotton from the cotton trees landing all around making it seem like snow. She caught a glimpse of a young eagle learning to fly. The strong wind making it difficult to maintain balance, unlike the rest of the experienced ones, she saw this one struggle a bit. But she loved to watch it take on the challenge. With a determination not to give up, but wanting to fly just like the rest of the group, despite the opposition from the strong wind trying to intimidate it, the young eagle tried to fly. Just as she was about to reach the mansion, Claudia tightened her bandage, it would not be right to throw it away yet. Her lie could be caught.

In a few days the routine started once again. Claudia was back to working in the mansion again with freedom. A few days later, Damiáno returned as well. Earlier than what was previously planned. Claudia kept this secret to herself without allowing Bula to sense it. They were back to their escapade at the ruins later that week. The gap had increased their longing for each other, which was reflected in the overwhelming fondness and affection they displayed in the early wintry morning. This time, Claudia had exercised extra caution while leaving the house, noiselessly.

Gleaners' fable

Each year, one day before the feast, Paklin Bai donated used stuff; men's shirts with partially broken buttons, empty liquor bottles and cans, aluminium vessels, plastic buckets, some without a handle, a small bamboo mat broken in the sides, and some window curtains, blankets, formal women's dresses and old books. Claudia's eyes fell on the bamboo mat, she could take it home and sleep all by herself, undisturbed, away from Mother, Jakin and Bula. That way, no one would notice her waking up early when she wanted to meet Damiáno, especially now that Bula, presumably, would be keeping a hawk-eye watch on her. Happily, Claudia brought the mat home; from now on, it was going to be her own little bedding, which she decided she would spread by the kitchen door.

The church feast was always a grand celebration in Oroshim; a solemn mass at church, solemnised by three priests in three different languages. In the homes; lavish cooking with relatives arriving from distant places for an overnight stay. Outside the churchyard, vendors would be selling things which are not otherwise available at the local bazaar. Kadiobodio, the sweetmeats made from jaggery and ginger, fresh and crunchy roasted grams, little trinkets like cross pendants, metallic bangles, yo-yo balls, toy whistles and toy dolls.

All of it would be followed by the tiatr staged on the night of the feast, the six to seven stage drama, the most sought after event of the village. Each of the acts would be bridged by one or two songs. Apart from which, the tiatr would have a typical story content; sadness, let-downs, frustrations, opposition, funny moments, romance, climax and the concluding happy-ever-after triumph.

'I will meet you tomorrow, Bab.' Claudia had told Damiáno when they parted in the morning at dawn. She had forgotten that the drama would be over much after midnight with the festive visitors awake almost through the night.

That morning in the backyard with her breakfast of black tea with some bread, she wished there was some way for her to tell him not to expect her the following day, realising the crowd would still be hovering around the village after the drama. She condemned herself for not having had the presence of mind to think that the morning of the feast night would be tough to meet up. Now there was no way she could convey the message to him. She sighed regretfully and sang the Gleaner's Fable to herself.

It was what the gleaners and reapers sang during harvest time to encourage themselves.

A song that narrated ancient fables that brought back energy and enthusiasm to continue with the long hours of hard work. Sometimes Gormai joined them in leading them to sing her favourite 'Kowdo the Chief.'

'Rise up son. Rise to your feet. Kowdo the chief is arriving. His voice, from the seas is approaching, as far as the skies. His voice alarms a sound of a twelve thousand strong army. Rise up son! Rise up to your feet. Kowdo the chief is arriving.

It was Gormai's soul song; probably she sang it for Father. The gleaners sang their favourite.

Sun is risen in the city of Rome; its rays have spread across the earth. Fly away peacock, now that you have hatched your eggs. The peacock hatched the eggs and flew away from the dirt.'

The field songs had ancient wisdom and a strange expression; a sarcasm, a thankfulness, an adoration, and if you deciphered the not so poetic lyrics of some songs, it had the unfolding of many hidden secrets. Tales of hard fought romance, a melancholy of a heartbreak, stories of loving and losing, a celebration of hard fought victory; the field songs had it all. The fable of the trespassing crow was one of Claudia's favourites.

'A crow was seeking shelter on a tree of purple sunbirds. The crow was a stranger in the sunbird pines, a pilgrim on his journey to Pathod, the distant plains.

The king of the pines, a hefty sunbird, chose to intimidate him. 'You are a house crow and near houses you must live; you'll look no good living on these coniferous trees.'

'If pines have joy, then let one be mine, for a day or two or three.'

'How could a good king permit a strange bird to dwell on a sunbird tree?'

The wise crow convinced the king to let him sojourn for a night or two.

Three days later, after a swift flight, the crow met the bird king that night.

'Let me, a few more nights.' The crow was found to plead.

'We live off rich nectars, but you on leftovers, else I would indeed.'

'Allow me to fly with you and I will find a leftover to catch.'

'Well! We fly in pairs, a black crow and a purple bird is never a match.'

'A little place to lie and away I fly.'

'Just a few more nights, not more than that.' The king decreed the request.

The following morning, when the sunbirds flew, two by two.

The crow despaired, 'Alas! If only I were one of you.'

Just then, a pretty feather tempted the crow to flap.

'Come!' She stretched to him, their wings overlapped.

She flew. He followed. He flew. She followed. And so they flew two by two.

'I wish I can fly forever with you.'

Soon the crow was caught pecking the sunbird beak to wing.

'Explain,' demanded the king.

'Your majesty, my tail got stuck, this gentleman helped.' The pretty sunbird lied, as she wept.

Wanting to lie no more,

when her new hatched babies resembled the crow.

'Flee now lest they find,' she cried.

'With you as my bride,' the crow replied.

Grasslands and plains, they flew with zest

building a cosy new nest;

No leftover bits nor nectar feed

They fed their young ones on berry seeds

No other sunbird in sight or a crow's drift,
Only a lonely expanse of the skies and seas.
In love; the brave crow and the pretty sunbird willed,
to raise a flock of a different breed.'

Claudia smiled and sighed again. Will it be a purple sunbird or a black crow or a different breed? She put on her feast dress, powdered her face, dipped a paper ribbon in water and dabbed her lips. Outside the church, people greeted each other with warm hugs and aggressive handshakes. Over three generations or more, parishioners had been a part of the church. Most seafarers took their annual break to celebrate the feast.

White shirt-black trouser clad men were all across the tent, some wore full suits and safaris, occupying the front pews. Women wore silky clothing and their special occasion jewellery. Food stalls with chourice pao, lemonade and beer were a part of the big cloth tent.

Delicacies like pork sorpotel, sannas, the toddy soaked rice cakes, arroz refogado, green beef curry, chicken xacuti replaced the daily curry and rice; a time of the year when the village folks sold home bred pigs, fowls and goats, days before the feast, and gathered enough money to shop for the feast day, most even borrowing.

Father sent Claudia to the nearest tavern to buy beer; sawdust covered ice blocks chilling multiple beer bottles outside every tavern. It was fondly rumoured that on this day there was more beer consumed than water drawn from the wells on an average day. A brief stop on the way and she watched the tiatr participants

get ready for the night's drama. Gonsal Irmao biting ginger to be able to sing clearly. Ti Santan practising dialogues for the evening's performance. Pakto Jose trying on his wife's bra for the woman's part that he was chosen for in the drama. The village didn't really have much respect for women choosing to take part in the drama. It was the men playing the woman's part, unless an outside actress, usually from Bombay, was brought in.

After getting back home, Claudia ground xacuti masala over the grindstone. Later, she helped Sankistao at the church kitchen. Post lunch, she helped Gormai carry the chilli, turmeric and onion stock she had bought for the whole year at the feast fair. All her efforts appreciated with a feast reward in cash from Gormai, Padkur and Sankistao. For most villagers of Oroshim, the real fun began at the end of the feast day; at the eagerly awaited tiatr. Spectators gathered early, to get the best seat under the temporary tent erected at the church compound by the local youth only for this night.

The tiatr began; local talent taking over the stage in the middle of loud cheering, clapping and whistles from the crowd. As usual there was a story with a break in between scenes for a song. The songs although crudely composed were a mirror to reflect the wrong deeds of the village folks. The drama was used as an instrument of indirect rebuke. The more controversial the story that was depicted in song and dialogue, the longer was its after-effect; usually remaining fresh on the minds of the viewers for days or even a month. Post interval, Claudia felt the restless anticipation reach its tempo. The audience in rapt silence at the story reaching a climax.

The sarcasm and rebuke expressed during the tiatr performance most often faced an immediate backlash, from individuals who were the target whose deeds were made public. It happened every year. Soon after the play ended, arguments would break out at the odd hours of the night. Often, they would lead to aggressive physical fights which would go on until dawn or until one of the fighting parties subdued the other. None of it interested Claudia, now that she had Damiáno to worry about, who would be waiting for her at the ruins, before dawn. If she didn't meet him, it would be breaking a promise which she had never done before, also it was hard to think of keeping a wonderful man like him waiting indefinitely. On the other hand, if she went to meet him, there was the possibility it might lead to trouble, with many of the village folk still around, even until sunrise.

'What's the time, Ti Jaki?' Claudia leaned forward to ask her elderly neighbour sitting in the front row with his wife.

'Two o'clock.' He answered in a hurry. No one liked getting disturbed during climax.

'Just two or is it past two?'

'Shhhhh. Keep quiet.' The neighbour retorted, his sudden shout disturbing the silence and drawing the entire audience attention towards Claudia. Almost on cue, as if that was not embarrassing enough, Bula, sitting adjacently, stomped Claudia's foot with hers. It stung Claudia badly but she got Bula's hint.

Under the circumstances there was no way Claudia could do anything but to go with the flow of the night and forget all about meeting Damiáno.

The accident

Claudia could hear Mother and Jakin in the kitchen, while she was still asleep. She jumped up when she suddenly realised the sun was already up and she had overslept. The tiatr and the predictable fights at night had ended up very late. Sankistao would be waiting. There was much work at the church kitchen. She hurried to get out of the house. The church compound was badly messed up after the feast. Scraps of paper, streamers and deflated balloons all around along with other litter, the bits and pieces left by the festive revellers. It took much time and effort to clean up and restore the neat sanctified look of the church premises. The utensils and used dishes had to be cleaned up too; quite a big heap. This is what usually accompanied special occasions celebrated at church; cutlery to clean, crockery to be washed and a lot of cleaning to do. Once done, Claudia ate the lunch that Sankistao offered; the remaining food from the feast.

It was late afternoon, by the time she was done with work. On the way back home, one of the workers in the field stopped her. 'Claudia, did you hear about the accident?' the worker asked. One couldn't always go by the villagers' blown-out-ofproportion news. They were known to stir storms in tea cups and turn moles into mountains.

'No,' Claudia replied, not wanting to pay any attention and encourage the possible rumour to spread.

'Do you think the Indians were behind it?'

'Maybe,' Claudia answered with disinterest and walked away. She had other things on her mind. Mother would be waiting to go to the big house to work and then Claudia had to come up with some way to convey to Damiáno; through a chit or perhaps a quick whisper, that it got impossible to meet him at the ruins the morning after the feast night.

'Let me know who it is. You are going there now, aren't you? It could be the older Bab or the younger Bab who died. I have to go and water the crop or I would go myself and see.'

Died? At the big house? Claudia stopped in her tracks. Astonished, she turned to look at the field worker walking away in another direction, leaving Claudia totally baffled with what she said. Claudia stood transfixed for a few moments, unable to react or to shout and call the worker back and ask her more.

Bab? Accident? Which Bab could it be? Not mine. No. No. Not possible. The voice screamed in her mind and her pulse began to race, as her breathing suddenly became rapid. Unable to form words, the mind just kept repeating the same thought in quick succession. Not my Bab. No. Please No. Her hands suddenly got clammy with sweat as she clenched them tightly and released a silent prayer from the deepest part of her being. A part of herself, reserved specially for Damiáno Bab. Her Damiáno Bab.

There were just two Babs at the big house. If the accident involved Damiáno Bab, that would be the most terrible thing she could ever encounter, she thought and tried to fight the enormity of the thing that welled up inside her mind. But if it was not Damiáno Bab, then it would be his father, Oliveira Bab, and that would be equally bad, she thought again, thinking of the distress it would cause Damiáno. The sudden shock gave way to a hitherto unknown fear which inspired her feet to move with speed and run with absolute abandon in the direction of the big house.

Jaku, their neighbour, was shutting down his tavern for the afternoon. It was a common practice all over Oroshim. It was time for their afternoon siesta which took pre-eminence over staying open and doing some business. 'I heard there was an accident at the big house. Do you know anything about it?' Claudia halted to ask, nostrils flared, out of breath, her eyes bulging. Jaku looked at her strangely, shrugged his shoulders and with a suspicious look said, 'I am not really sure, heard it's a fall.'

Claudia immediately pulled up her long skirt and began running again. Her speed got her to the mansion faster than what was usually possible. Reaching the mansion gate, she slowed down to catch her breath; her heart was thumping fast. Panting, sweaty and anxious, she pushed herself inside and saw a crowd gathered. And as she pushed through the crowd, she saw him. Damiáno! He was lying on a wooden sofa wrapped in blood soaked bandages inside Paklin Bai's sitting room. One look at his bloody sight as he lay immobile on the sofa, had an overpowering effect on her. Claudia looked around to observe what was going on and tried to make more sense of the situation. Her mind and heart were at war; she just couldn't get a hold on her feelings. She observed some Portuguese officials were in animated conversation with an even more animated Oliveira Bab. Two of them had a stethoscope hanging down their necks. Mother was peeping from behind the curtain. Paklin Bai sat on a chair next to the sofa, quiet but disturbed, her red puffy eyes fixed on Damiáno's body. The crowd looked shocked, mumbling in hushed whispers, they cast sympathetic glances at each of the Oliveiras in turns.

Then suddenly, from the corner of her eye she noticed something that made her gasp in amazement. As if in a trance or in a dream, she pushed herself closer to where Damiáno lay. She wished desperately that what she had just seen was true and paused for a moment to look at his body closely. She was sure she was right. With an excitement that could not be explained she screamed out, 'He is alive. Doctor, Paklin Bai, Oliveira Bab. He is alive. I saw him move. He's not dead.' Claudia screamed loudly, tears rolling through her sobs.

'Take the girl away.' Oliveira Bab commanded. Someone pulled Claudia, away, towards the kitchen. Mother joined them, followed by Paklin Bai who reached out her hand to touch Claudia. 'Damiáno Bab is alright. We shouldn't disturb him, he is hurt and needs rest. Now go do your work.' She said to Claudia, softly.

That dialogue from Paklin Bai calmed Claudia down like a bucket of ice cold water suddenly thrown over the head. Now armed with calmness, Claudia went about doing the things she always did at the big house. Even Mother's angry expression, each time she looked at her throughout the evening didn't bother her. The last thing on Claudia's mind for the remaining part of the day was that she had made a complete fool of herself. The presence of the Portuguese doctors, the silence in the house, Oliveira Bab's upset expression, all of it was reminding her of her public blunder.

The sun was ready to go down the green horizon turning dark as it sank lower and lower behind the distant trees. Work at the mansion was done. Claudia and Mother were on their way home. An unusual silence separated them, unlike every other day where there was a lot of womanly chatter between the two. Through the silence Claudia's mind started working up questions again. Was Mother angry because Claudia had made a fool of herself at Paklin Bai's house or did Bula discuss something with her while she was away at the church?

Although tempted to ask, she chose not to speak in the open about anything concerning their family. Nature has ears, she had heard the village elders say. Bula and Jakin were chatting at the backyard, warming themselves with the fire lit up to heat water for a bath. Claudia followed Mother and went inside.

'Mother, the kerosene is less in the bottle and the lamp is empty, is there more kerosene?' Claudia blurted out, intending to break the silence between them. As she stood over the cooking bowls, warming up food for the night, Mother replied, in a low tone,

'There's a full kerosene bottle behind the tins. Take it out.'

Mother then put off the fire, covered the cooking bowls with aluminium covers and came towards Claudia, her eyes slanting towards the backyard to make sure the other two girls didn't hear what she had to say. 'Claudia, why did you react like that at the big house, there were so many people around. And you know that it was an embarrassment.'

'Mother, I thought Damiáno Bab was....'

'What? Dead?'

Claudia nodded, her troubled eyes displaying some of the previous shock.

'Claudia, I want you to tell me the truth. Did you ever spend time alone with Damiáno Bab, anytime?'

Claudia nodded her head in approval.

'And ... what exactly happened?'

Claudia remained silent.

'What happened between the two of you? You have to tell me Claudia. Did you let him touch you?' Mother insisted.

'Mother, just sometimes. But ...' Claudia broke down, not really wanting to confess it all to Mother.

But Mother had got the point and narrowed her eyes with an alas-my-child-not-you-too expression. An expression that was seen on her face when Bula and Jakin did the wrong thing.

Mother went silent for a moment then turned to shut the kitchen door, leaving Bula and Jakin outside.

'Claudia, we are just servants in that house. Look at what happened to Bula and Jakin; they could have been well settled in life with a good man, if only they had a little more self control and patience. I thought you were more sensible. I'm really shocked and disappointed. Now I want you to get what I'm saying once and for all in that head of yours. We cannot go to the mansion for any other reason but to work and to earn money. That's it. And does anyone else know about this? Gormai or Sankistao or anybody?'

Claudia briskly shook her head in the negative, a sheepish expression in her eyes and guilt on her face.

'Good that they don't. None of them is to ever know of it. Do you hear me Claudia?' she thundered close to Claudia's ears.

'Yes Mother. I understand.'

'Who knows, by now they must be talking about you. I certainly hope you haven't raised their suspicion with your display today. Don't you think they will wonder as to why a servant girl started crying? Well, it's just that she imagined that her master was dead. So what? What would she cry so desperately for? As though she had lost one of her own family members?' she continued. 'Claudia, I'm telling you today, let anyone die, it has nothing to do with us, are we in a position to help anyone or change anything? Living in this village is not as simple as you think. No point in getting too emotional. Let him die.'

'Mother, that's wicked, that's not good, please don't talk like that,' Claudia pleaded.

'This Sunday Piedade Ferrao will be in town. You have to prepare yourself to meet their family. And don't you do any work in the mansion bedrooms without telling me, do you hear me?'

'Yes Mother. I understand.'

'Now go open the kitchen door and light the lantern, it's dark in the front room.'

Poili

Claudia ate two mugs full of millet and rice porridge; the secret diet responsible for the extra stamina and vitality among the field workers. Everyone in the village called the porridge *magic porridge*. It was also a go to diet when someone felt weak or sickly. But it was a diet that was enjoyable, not something to detest.

Mother was behaving strict at home to make sure the girl-seeing was done without incident for Claudia with the Ferrao's family. She was ready to do anything to make sure Claudia got married to the most eligible bachelor, Piedade Ferrao.

Claudia hummed a love song:

'*My strong man has gone to the seas*
And now my heart aches for his return
As my love departed into the waters
He has promised to pack a fifty kisses in a bottle.'

The people in Oroshim enjoyed singing, they sang loudly, without restraint at any time without any reason. In their homes, at the fields, while walking the lanes, while sitting at a balcao. The toddy tapper sang as he dangled on tall coconut tree trunks on his way to tap toddy and the bread man sang as he pedalled his bicycle from one purchase to the next. Everyone in the village exercised a unique freedom to express themselves through songs.

Strangely the romance that was so powerfully expressed through music was not encouraged in real life for unmarried folk. That privilege belonged only to the married couples.

Drama awaited Claudia at home on her return from working at the church one day. Bula was profusely crying, angry at being stopped by Matil Mashen, the bar lady to whom Father owed money. It was not unusual. It was one of the methods used by the lenders to recover their money from borrowers on *poili*, the first of the month. Though, *poili*, in Konkani meant the first of the month, the word had a twist. *Poili* was supposed to be pockets-full, the day that people received their salaries. It was a once-in-a-month day, when the market place turned into a seller's paradise. Children had their choicest foods, ice-fruits, toffees and cola. The empty wooden tavern drawers were now filled with money collected from two sources; the money from regular drinkers who borrowed money from anywhere they could, as well as the money that came from the customers receiving money either as salary or for a completed project or work. On *poili*, most homes had enough good food. No compromised meals of salt fish or pickles, instead, fresh fish and meat was plentiful at every mealtime. The abundance lasted less than a week, then, within days, things bounced back to the way they were. Poili was a day the debtors paid back their creditors. Not Claudia's Father though. With no income coming in, he had failed to pay again. That's when their feni selling neighbour had rudely stopped

Bula, intentionally, thinking the embarrassment would help in recovering her money. Bula was on her way to the tailor's house. Bula had cried; unfortunately none of those emotions worked on the feni sellers, at least not on the *poili*.

Claudia and Mother would get their month's pay for working at the mansion when Paklin Bai would pay them in the afternoon on every first day of the new month, without fail. This was one thing that Mother really appreciated about the Oliveiras. Watching Bula cry, Claudia was moved.

She decided to use whatever little money she had saved from the money she received from working at Paklin Bai's mansion to pay off Father's debt to Matil Mashen. She unfolded the handkerchief that was tied in knots, hidden behind Father's old books.

She counted the money and stepped out with Bula as instructed by Mother. Matil Mashen wasn't the only one that Father owed money to. Over time, he frequented many different taverns; Casa Mingu, Casa de Antok, Domingo Tavern, Jaku's tavern and of course Matil Mashen's. The girls would have to visit these places and find out if Father owed any money to them; that way they could save themselves from the embarrassment of being stopped publicly.

'So is your Bab alright now?'

In her mind, Claudia knew that Bula would manipulate the talk and somehow it would end up in an argument. So she chose to ignore Bula's question, as they walked along silently.

'Damiáno Bab returned earlier than expected but you didn't let me know. Very clever.'

'I didn't even know he was back from Daman, when I did, he was with injuries, all bandaged.'

'You expect me to believe those lies?'

'Alright, if you don't want to believe, fine. Bula I am telling you there is too much work at the big house. With Damiáno Bab recovering on bed, the bed sheets need to be changed daily. Special food has to be prepared for him without oil and spices, and then his daily dressing ritual. There is a lot of work.' Claudia said in an attempt to discourage Bula from thinking of going to the mansion.

'You know you only increase the impression of your cunningness and stupidity when you try to convince someone with too much talk. I don't promise much. But I am telling you, once he gets better; I am going to the big house and that same day you, my dear will stop going there or try meeting him.'

'I promise you I will tell you as soon as he is well.'

'Fine. But, try fooling me this time and you will regret it.'

Claudia stayed silent. At the moment, she just had to agree to everything that Bula said, and pretend that she is serious about every promise she was making. After the payment for Father's liquor was done, Claudia and Bula took a short cut through Gormai's house to get to the big house. Bula didn't get along much with Gormai, she stopped for a moment, greeted Gormai and left. Sitting in the balcao, Gormai was leisurely drawing in her Idi puffs. 'Claudia, did your mother tell you that Piedade's family wants to have a girl-seeing,' Gormai asked as though it was a closely guarded secret.

'Yes, she did. Gormai, I need to go. Paklin Bai will be waiting. I'll be back here in the evening just before tea time.'

'Don't forget my dear, it's a once in a life opportunity for you and I want us to be well prepared for the proposal. And how is the Oliveira's son doing? I hear he nearly died in an accident?'

'He must be better. We didn't get any news about him since yesterday. I am going there now.'

'Bring your mother along in the evening, I want to talk to her,' Gormai told her.

Claudia had to interrupt, her mind preoccupied with thoughts of Damiáno. Excusing herself, Claudia left Gormai's house to hurry to the big house. Nothing was as important as knowing that Damiáno was well. Gormai's words renewed her concern for Damiáno. 'Nearly died?' That's how the villagers hyperbolise things, making a four out of a one, that's how the locals termed it. One couldn't always go by their exaggerated information. It was what had made her react and cry out at the big house.

Claudia filled the bathing water pot, when she reached the mansion. Mother had not arrived yet. 'Claudia, you're already here? Good, Listen! Damiáno Bab is sleeping, so keep the noise low.'

'Paklin Bai. Is there any danger to Damiáno Bab's health?'

'Not at all, he is feeling much better already. Doctor said he needs rest, a few days of healthy diet, medicine on time, and Bab will be fine. Alright? Now go do your work, but peacefully. We don't want to disturb Bab, do we?'

When Mother entered, she displayed almost a similar concern when she enquired with Paklin Bai about Damiáno, just that Mother's concern was not as genuine. Claudia heard as Mother faked it too much, especially when she told Paklin Bai that she could not sleep all night worrying about Damiáno Bab's condition. It was plain talk, done within the community, which Mother continued with Paklin Bai without even bothering about their effect.

Father dies

Father breathed his last in Jakin's arms.

It was an honour for Jakin. The village believed that if a person died in someone's arm, the deceased had greater love and respect for that person over others.

An hour back, Jakin had tried to make Father drink some water, Mother had unbuttoned his shirt to let him breathe better. Nothing worked. Claudia was constantly yelling at Mother to call Doctor Kasim, the village doctor. Mother kept putting it off.

In Oroshim the folks often said that Dr Kasim's hand was good; Mother probably hesitated because of his high consultation charges. Besides, Doctor Kasim, it was known, would require a new soap to wash hands after examining the sick; a clean towel, and then a cup and saucer for his tea.

Two days back, when Father was drunk at the bullfight, in the church square field, he had openly ridiculed Jakin. Father had called her every cuss word anyone could possibly use in their drunkenness. He called her embarrassing names claiming that she had shamed the entire family. The fuddled drama had garnered more attention than the bull fight. As curious onlookers grinned amused, Jakin tried as best not to react, putting up a brave expression but only as long as she was at the church square. Reaching home, as soon as she saw Mother's face, she broke down, like fizz from the bottled soda bursting out when shaken. Helpless, Mother watched her cry bitterly.

Father's drinking had to be stopped, somehow. The next day she decided to attempt, what she had considered before. She had tried many things, except this. She had heard stories among the village women how this crude, irregular remedy had stopped their men from excessive drinking. It was a strange remedy of squeezing the head of a particular breed of fish into the alcoholic drink. She remembered the smiling faces of the women who shared their successful secret after it worked. But she also recollected the remorse filled looks on the faces of women who tried the same remedy with drastic consequences.

Suddenly remembering, Mother rushed to put the kitchen fire off. Generally, there would be no cooking for the day in the house where there was a death. Claudia followed her and summoned the courage to ask. 'Mother, did you try to give Father the fish....'

'Shsshh quiet,' She jumped and clamped her hand over Claudia's mouth, stifling her.

'What??? Mother!!!!' exclaimed Claudia stunned to see the look of fear in Mother's eyes and face.

'Keep quiet Claudia, don't be foolish. I thought it would work.' Mother admitted softly.

'But Mother, we spoke of the dangers of that remedy...'

'Hm, yes, we did. I know it was a foolish thing to do. Which woman in her right mind would set her own self up to become a widow. I don't know what to do now.' Mother blurted out with agony written all over her face and hysteria swelling up in her voice.

'Claudia ...'

'Mother ...'

A stony silence accompanied their emotion charged discourse. Dazed, both of them remained silent, stoic in the kitchen as though waiting, hoping that somebody would come to their rescue, magically. Unknowingly Mother was clutching tightly at Claudia's right hand, causing pain, but this time the pain in the heart overshadowed the pain in the hand as Claudia clutched Mother's hand in return as they both wondered what to do.

It was an ignorant, unintentional mistake from Mother, though the village elders would never look at it that way. They would holler *crime* at the top of their voice. It was, technically. They stood glaring at the possibility of being ostracised from the village community; there was already enough against them to lose face and their place in the strict society they lived in. A decision had to be made. A careful decision. Well considered. Taking into account all the possible outcomes, a wise decision had to be made before announcing Father's death to anyone.

And just when the silence seemed to be the best cover, Bula gave out a piercing loud scream that rang out and tore into the silence.

It brought the neighbours rushing in along with Gormai who began crying before reaching their door. Mother broke herself free from Claudia and rushed to get close to Bula in crying loudly, accompanied by Jakin.

One by one the villagers entered. Glaring at the women. Huddled together. Gormai beating her chest in between loud sobs, screaming, 'What happened to my son, somebody tell me? Why is he gone so cold? When did this happen? How? What did you do to him?' she questioned, holding Claudia's shoulders and shaking her for an answer. It was the typical village pattern that accompanied most death announcements. Such display of emotion from a person outside the immediate family often overwhelmed the bereaved family.

'Fever. He had high fever,' Claudia blurted out.

'And why didn't you tell me about it when you came home yesterday? I would have come and swabbed his body with wet cloth, given him some kanji, done something,' Gormai howled.

'Mother tried some of those remedies, Gormai.'

'What, Busha?' Gormai asked, turning angrily towards Mother, demanding an explanation from her daughter-in-law. Another of the typical behaviours demonstrated by mothers-in-law in the village.

'I thought it was a mild fever,' Mother said, unable to meet Gormai's penetrating gaze.

'So you left him to die?'

'No Gormai. How could we? Mother was with him all the time. And Jakin kept applying wet cloth to his head all night. The fever had come down, for a while, but in the morning....' Claudia's mouth trembled as she spoke hoping to calm Gormai; it worked. Gormai stopped questioning, weeping instead and began praising her son through soft sobs and streams of steady tears. After a few moments, Gormai got hold of herself and got busy planning out the ceremonial customs to be followed. She first arranged some of the neighbours to bathe and dress the body in a set of clean clothes.

The large church bell tolled with the death knell. Three times, three slow strokes, echoing a painful tune far and wide. Everyone within hearing distance immediately knew what it meant and whispered a silent prayer, first for the bereaved family and then a silent prayer of thanks to God that they were spared. As the news spread, villagers came in one by one, and those present whispered to the new curious visitors that it was due to high fever.

Towards evening, the house was rearranged. Father's washed and dressed body was placed inside a wooden coffin which was placed inside the house, resting on two wooden stools on either side. The men stayed outside, the women remained inside. Every time a new visitor arrived to offer condolences there would be a sudden breakout of crying from all the women, accompanied by a sudden calm. The ebb and flow, weeping and silence continued through the next day, but as the time for the funeral drew closer, the scene altered. When strongly built men came in to carry the body out of the house, the noise of crying reached a sudden crescendo; everybody wailed loudly, at the same time, relatives, neighbours, friends, acquaintances, even strangers gathered out of curiosity, some out of compassion, as it was customary to show respect to any family grieving the death of a loved one. Someone had arranged for a brass band to accompany the funeral procession. The band was led through the streets by a professional mourner, who led the crowd. The bereaved accompanied the casket, while other members of the funeral procession followed slowly as the crowd wound its way through the streets en route to the body's final resting place. As the solemn music blared through the trumpets and the painful beats of the big drum sounding the funeral tunes rang out, the sound of crying increased tremendously, as if the trumpets and drums had signalled an alert.

The procession of mourners wound its way through the bunds towards the church where the funeral would take place. The men dressed in red and white lifted the coffin and placed it in the grave. One by one, friends and neighbours arrived to offer condolences; they hugged and planted soft kisses on each cheek, then they stopped for a moment to praise the dead and tell the loved ones how sad and sympathetic they felt about their loss. The formalities consumed much time and the funeral was tiresome for the grieving family.

At the cemetery, flowers were showered; people sobbed, some aloud, some soft, some in pretence for it was shameful to be spotted with dry eyes, especially for relatives. Mother knew that crying aloud and wailing uncontrollably was considered to be a sign of genuine mourning. *Fever. Fever. Fever.* She kept chanting one word. 'Tell Mother to keep quiet; this sounds like drama.' Claudia whispered in Bula's ears.

Her mother's act reminded Claudia of the men who dress up as women in Intruz plays at carnival time. They do not bother about their moustaches or beards and go ahead with their female roles. Worse still, they would not bother if people believed in their comic act as they desperately tried to make people laugh at their chaste humour. Gross overacting. Mother was doing it now.

What if someone concluded that her fever-fever song was fake? If they did, it would be trouble for the family. It angered Claudia; since yesterday she had been losing temper over small issues.

Claudia saw Bula move closer to Mother and whisper in her ear; Mother sheepishly looked at Claudia and went quiet. Mother had her own fears; she knew people would laugh at her and gossip if she didn't cry enough. The village was judgmental.

Claudia and her sisters were also supposed to cry, but Claudia had not shed a tear. She resented whatever had happened, knowing that it only worsened their predicament, yet she had to keep quiet, hold her peace.

The ambience in the cemetery was typical. Candles and flowers; men assisting in the funeral ceremony in red and white capes; some men in white shirts and black trousers, the women in either plain black or just black and white ...

Bula, Jakin and Claudia had not much of black and white clothing. Though elderly women always insisted that a girl should have at least one set of white blouse and a black skirt, the sisters didn't have anything in black or white. Those were colours for rare occasions like funerals and church service during Lent. Bula had borrowed a skirt and blouse from Lourdina. Jakin wore Mother's old worn out black dress. Claudia was the odd one out but it didn't seem to bother her much to attend the funeral in the purple blouse and matted blue skirt that Paklin Bai had given her some months back.

Paklin Bai and Oliveira Bab were present at the funeral. Damiáno was out of town. The helpers handed out a handful of mud to Mother, to Gormai, and then to Jakin, Bula, and Claudia.

She held her fist tight, refusing to take it. It didn't mean anything to her. How would throwing mud help? It wouldn't bring Father back. She was hurting inside. She missed him. It was the first time she didn't bother about the villagers gossiping about her.

She watched others shower flowers, colourful, vibrant petals scattering over the coffin as it was lowered into the grave. She hated the custom of throwing a handful of mud over the grave. Loved ones had to start, the rest would follow one by one. It was a sign of respect. Claudia could not relate to the kind of respect that came from throwing of mud. It was the final custom of the funeral, the final goodbye from those who cared, a handful of mud.

Yes, from those who cared. Who cared for Father? He had lost it all.

People hugged Claudia, consoling her. Once or twice her angry gaze shifted to Mother. Balancing between two old graves, she stood loathing the formalities and customs. She would have preferred to be alone, no one to hug her, no one to console her, no one to come close to her. It was not going to help. No hug could comfort her now.

Sankistao tried opening her fist. She didn't move. Padre Jose, Ti Botelho, Karmin Timai, and many others tried, but Claudia stood firm like a statue.

'Somebody should help the girl to cry,' they said.

Claudia could neither cry nor move. Her eyes were fixed on the grave and her feet firmly crushing the small plants and weeds protruding out of the cemetery mud. More and more people hugged her, offering advice, comforting words, sweet mournful condolences. Some even came and wiped her eyes with their little handkerchiefs though there were no tears to wipe.

As the evening grew darker, the funeral crowd began to disappear, in groups of threes and fours, walking back to the house of mourning. Some women held Jakin, some Bula, some held Gormai, some threw their arms around Mother, and some led Claudia carefully through the bunds. Wordless, expressionless, Claudia allowed them to take her back home.

She refused the cup of tea that was brought to her by the woman helping in the kitchen. People walked in and out of their house. The neighbourhood ladies brought provisions from their homes, and as was customary, cooked in the house of death.

The house was full and buzzed with the women's hushed chatter. Men continued to arrive, to sit outside to signify their presence and show respect, many had a look of genuine concern. Padre Jose sent a messenger with the word that the elders would be visiting soon to do the customary rosary. Elders like Luis Bakaar, Ti Botelho and many others.

Jakin joined Claudia in the backyard and handed her a mug of kanji. 'Take this, it is not too hot. Drink!' Claudia neither moved nor took the mug from her sister. Jakin flopped on the ground, silent, just like her little sister. The sisters sat in silence for a while together, the tin mug of rice kanji still in Jakin's hand. 'This is getting cold,' Jakin said breaking the silence.

Claudia looked straight at her sister but said nothing.

'So ...' Jakin sobbed. Claudia did not cry, even if she tried she knew she wouldn't be able to. Something hard sat upon her chest.

'Padre Jose said he is coming with the elders in a short while for the rosary. It's time for Mother to confess the truth,' Jakin said as she blew her nose.

'Did she say that?' Claudia spoke at last.

'Hmm. She did.'

'Tell the truth to the elders?'

'She has to, Claudia,' Jakin responded.

'Please call Mother, please.'

'Are you feeling alright?'

'Call Mother!' Claudia's nostrils flared.

Jakin rushed inside and came out with Mother to the backyard, Bula beside them.

'Here. Have some water; you don't have anything in your stomach since yesterday,' Mother said, offering Claudia a mug full of water.

Claudia grasped her mother's hand and dragged her to the pig sty where no one could see them in the deepening dusk. Jakin and Bula followed them. The pig sty was deserted and dark, it smelled foul.

'Did you tell Jakin you are going to confess and tell the truth to the elders now?'

'Claudia, we have never hidden anything from the villagers, you know the rules here.'

'Who cares about rules, Mother? You are not telling them the truth.'

'Don't. Claudia. Don't make it difficult on Mother. She is right, we must confess like we have always done with all our mistakes,' Jakin protested.

'Mistake. You think they will call it mistake. They will say she killed him.'

'People will say things, child. Let them. They have said it in the past and they will say it now. Who knows, maybe they will say things about us as long as we are alive? Our times are bad,' Mother started crying helplessly.

'Mother, no! Don't tell it to them.'

'Claudia, what's wrong with you?' Jakin argued.

'You keep your mouth shut, Jakin. That's all you should do now, and tell this duck's bottom too,' Claudia looked at Bula.

'I will not tell anyone,' Bula assured, for once not reacting to Claudia's comment. Claudia was like a littering lioness; nobody could mess with her in this mood.

'Mother, look at me. We don't have much left now, we all agree. But listen, the very little that we are left with will also be snatched away from us.'

'Like what?' Jakin intervened again.

'Like what? Like working at Paklin Bai's house. Working in the church kitchen. Piedade Ferrao, you said it will be a dream come true, didn't you? Piedade Ferrao is your dream, isn't he, Mother? None of it will exist for us any longer. Not our jobs, not our house. It's Father's house. You and Father built it for us to live in. You think they care? They won't let us stay. One carelessness. One confession. It's the truth, but don't tell it to them. We have told them enough. Did it help? They won't let us live in peace.'

'Don't you know I know it all, Claudia?'

'Then why, Mother?'

'I'll do it. You tell me what I should do and I'll do it.'

'Just keep the secret. For my sake. Please. They are miserable folks, these elders.'

'I won't. You don't worry, child,' Mother assured her.

Claudia's nostrils widened, tears began to form in her eyes. She panted and sniffed, and then the tears came rolling down her cheeks. She howled. Mother looked at her and like a mirror image, did exactly as she saw her daughter do. Jakin and Bula followed suit.

Their tears sprang from the deep rooted pain of years of humiliation, loss, sorrow, and Father's death.

The cries were also cries of mourning. Father was gone. The man they had once put all trust into was gone. The irony of it all was that he was gone without doing much about the trust they had put in him. It should not have been a loss at all, but they still mourned his death. They could not help it. They loved him.

The neighbourhood women who were working in the kitchen, the men sitting outside for the rosary to begin, everybody rushed to the pig sty. The elders were approaching, they said. Claudia, Jakin, Bula and Mother continued to cry out loud. In a way it impressed the villagers. In Oroshim loved ones were appreciated for mourning over the dead, it would be discussed for days; they would debate who cried the most, then express sympathy towards the one who cried the most, all the while repeating the stock phrase, 'Don't cry.' The person who didn't cry much would be looked down upon.

Mother, Claudia, Bula and Jakin were pampered as they sat for the customary rosary. Gormai, Lourdina and her family, the neighbours, Father's old friends, Mother's old friends from the balcao days, Sankistao, the priests, the elders; they were all present in Claudia's home.

Half way through the rosary the sniffing and the sobbing subsided. The rosary was over. Slowly, one by one, people began to leave. The elders sat a while to comfort the family.

The elders spoke of Father again. 'We will miss our brother,' they said. Mother thanked them in her exaggeratedly humble tone. The elders left with an assurance to be there for the family at all times.

'I don't know what to say about this fever. It could be the start of an epidemic. Take care. Eat well,' Luis Bakaar advised.

The elders left.

There was peace at last.

Queijo de leite

Two bad things had happened, too quick and unexpected, almost around the same time. Father's death and Damiáno's accident, both of which had barred Claudia's chances of meeting Damiáno, the way she did in the past months. A third thing had happened, but it wasn't bad, it was a good thing, at least in comparison to the bad things. Piedade Ferrao's family was considering Claudia to be one of the prospective matches for their only son. 'What great news it would be, thought Claudia, had it not been.... anyway.' She stopped her worrying thoughts right there. She had to keep her father's only wish in mind; to see one of the girls being married and well settled. Everything that happened in recent times was bogging down to one decision; marry Piedade Ferrao.

Lately, Claudia had found herself doing her chores for the sake of it. The past few days were brutal to devour a lot of her joy. Paklin Bai needed buffalo milk to make Queijo de leite, the exotic-cheese she would make once in a while. Claudia walked all the way to Tukaram's farm. The old batch of milk was over so Claudia had to wait a while until Tukaram milked his second batch of buffaloes. The cattle shed smelled foul, as Tukaram, dressed in his checkered loin cloth milked the buffaloes. He poured fresh milk in overflowing steel tumblers. She waited in silence, the farm bringing in fresh memories of intimate time spent with Damiáno, where they rode to, Damiáno loving her right on the damp hay of the haystack. Tukaram even gave her a generous quarter litre of free milk, she took it uttering a humble God-do-good-to-you; the typical way Goans thanked.

A loud whistling tune drew Claudia's attention to the coconut tree, another loin cloth clad neighbour, Bostiao the toddy tapper, was climbing down with a toddy container and sickle. He stopped Claudia and offered her fresh toddy, she declined it, being no big fan of the palm toddy. Many in the village, especially men, enjoyed its intoxicating flavour. The liquid was better off to leaven the rice cakes, the main use of the toddy, she thought. The behaviour of her village folk amused her. The hearts of the village folk would move on two occasions; if one had a tragedy in the family or if one had something big to show off. People in the middle, with a normalcy, with no tragedy or greatness to flaunt had no attention from the village. She would have loved to take the toddy home for Father, but nobody had offered it when he was alive. The local proverb saying, the dead cow gave twelve litres of milk was apt in such a situation. That was the thing, most people waited to be kind to someone until the person was dead and gone, speaking good about him and showing love when he was no more.

Mother was already at the big house. Paklin Bai started her cheese-making. The boiling milk bubbled vigorously; Paklin Bai added lemon juice to it and asked Mother to take the vessel off the fire. A few more teaspoons of lemon juice separated the milk solids into nice lumps and a pale green liquid showed up. Paklin Bai drained the liquid before putting up the cheese in the bamboo crafted moulds, the *quejinha*. After sprinkling salt, the Queijo de leite was allowed to stand a while.

As Mother and Claudia were leaving, Paklin Bai gave them some of the cheese to take home. She also gave some money for the black dresses since the custom of the village demanded that people wear black only, after a family member's death. Padkur had given Claudia money to buy some black material too and Sankistao towards the stitching charges.

The following Saturday evening, the three sisters—Jakin, Bula and Claudia went to Lojeir Naik, the cloth merchant, by local transport. The girls found themselves giggling through the ride, suddenly aware that it wouldn't be good if anyone saw them smiling. No member of a mourning family was supposed to laugh or smile publicly, like the way they did. They would be gossiped about. But, the girls were in a good mood; it wasn't often that they sat in paid transport, stepped out to shop with enough money in hand. How could any girl about to enter Naik's cloth shop not express happiness? Zig zag lace, cute buttons, plain pitch black brassieres and petticoats, plain white brassieres and petticoats and a variety of colourful cloth materials; there was so much that one could shop for, but for now, the girls were happy to buy at least the black cloth, which they were supposed to.

Father's sudden, unexpected death was still dominant, fresh. Although the girls had grown without being expressive of each other's emotions, they had lived together long enough to empathise without vocalising it. What brought a shift in their attitude could be attributed to the absence of a dominant male in a house full of females, the utter uncertainty of their future, the rude strangeness of Father's death, another careless mistake which led to a loss of life and not just loss of respect, the fear of harbouring the secret; all of these and much more that cannot be expressed accompanied their daily life, carrying its own unavoidable stress.

The realisation that they were now left with nothing but each other to endure life ahead, began to break boundaries that were previously unseen, it started to bridge the distance that had earlier separated their closeness.

They now realised that they would need to rely on each other's strength and draw comfort from one another to face life with boldness. Now was the time to forge a bond which replaced the loud arguments, uncaring rude behaviour and selfish fighting.

At Naik's cloth shop, they bought cloth sufficient enough to stitch two black dresses for each other as well as for Mother. A little portion of money was still left out of which they bought a bottle of cola to share among the three of them and saved some amount to commute back in paid public transport again. All that extra spending would of course remain a secret only among the three of them.

Claudia didn't have to be reminded of that date; it was on her mind every day, for some time now. The date was the 2 December, as a conscious thought or even as a heart-skipping-beats reminder, a day prior to the girl-seeing at Ferrao's house.

For the past few days, she had been spending a lot of time with Gormai. Each instance she spent time with Gormai, she seemed to have convinced Claudia that marrying Piedade was going to be the best decision of her life.

The sky was a sheet of clear blue; no lightning, no thunder, no downpours, no clouds. It was calm and peaceful, unlike the season just gone by. Yet the season gone by had left a visible mark all around. The meadows were turned lush green, the ponds were filled, grass covered the hills and mountains, the fields were full. Everything seemed energised. Recharged. Stronger.

The abundant rain water flowed from the mountain top down to the hillocks, slithering through the backwaters, like it did each year. There at the backwaters the cattle were taken to graze and to be bathed; the ancient village folk had passed on a legacy of praise concerning the rains, they called it the season of sustenance. However, it was the winter that belonged to many celebrations in Oroshim. A lot happened during this chill season; the church feast, paddy harvest yielding rice, Christmas; the sweet smell of food and tasty treats filled the village air during this season.

'It's a good day to collect dry leaves,' Gormai mumbled to herself as she and Claudia walked up the hills. Claudia walked along silently; the breeze ruffling her hair; she enjoyed that warm afternoon breeze. The sun was bright, the hill was steep and the stream surrounded by a variety of washed clothes spread out for drying by the village folk. With most people taking their daily nap around this time of day, late afternoons were usually quieter; Claudia enjoyed working in that kind of undisturbed silence.

Dry leaves and sticks lay in plenty at the hilltop, which made for good fuel to heat up bathing water, especially during winters when everyone preferred hot water baths. Gormai had carried two large empty sacks. Sweeping with the help of a coconut sheath as a broomstick, Claudia gathered it all into a big heap before pushing it into the sacks. Once both sacks were full, Claudia walked up to Gormai, sitting on an elevated mound of red mud. She had already prepared her cigar by rolling long tobacco leaves inside a flat berry leaf. Examining the full sacks from a distance, Gormai tucked the match box back into her sari blouse. 'Do you have a good dress for the chapel feast?' she asked.

'When is it?' Claudia questioned back, pretending she didn't know about it.

'Tomorrow. I knew your Mother would forget to tell you. That woman is always in a dream or what?'

'Mother did tell me. It is the date that slipped my mind, Gormai.'

Smoking half the cigar and leisurely blowing out a few smoke rings through her mouth, Gormai announced with a proud smile. 'We will be spending the day at Ferrao's house.'

Claudia wiped little sweat drops from her brow, ignoring the sharp, anxiety filled sensation inside her. It had been happening lately; a strange pang, mostly when she thought of Damiáno. 'The chapel feast has a big fair, isn't it Gormai? I hear they have fake chains and rings that look like gold. How I wish I can get one chain for myself.'

'The feast fair will always be there, that's not our purpose though. The Ferrao family will be seeing you for the first time, we better focus on that part. We will go straight for the mass then join them at their house for lunch. Their daughter will be there too. That girl is well settled with the only son of a bakaar; a large house and a big stretch of land. I hear she was given a seven-fold trousseau as part of her dowry. Most well-to-do people give in five folds. Imagine! Seven sets of blouses, saris, dresses, undergarments, shoes, and heaven alone knows how much more they gave her during the marriage. The Ferraos are not less in fortune. The family house is big. The house is built with cement, not mud, mind you. No country tiles, the roof has only Mangalore tiles and the flooring is of red cement. You are to get a chance to settle in there, child. Piedade is their only son. All you do is live in the abundance! No cow dung to spread every now and then, no need to draw well water in pots, they have servants to do that work. You have worked enough through the years; I am telling you this is the right thing for you, Claudia,' Gormai continued calmly. 'Only keep in mind that they all will be watching you, so don't behave silly. You are a wise girl and you should not miss this lifetime opportunity to get chosen for a well to do household like the Ferrao's,' Gormai advised, tapping the last bit of the simmering cigar ash with her forefinger. Claudia remained silent in deep thought, and Gormai spoke again. 'You are a strange girl, so much like your father. Any girl would blush to hear this, look at you; no trace of a smile or a shy laughter.'

Claudia turned toward Gormai, her tone and expression serious as she looked for an answer for the question she just asked Gormai. 'You'll do well. It is a holy sacrament. One must learn to protect it and cherish it, takes a strong heart to make a fine marriage. Listen to me girl, when a man does something good, you need a heart to smile for him. When he is bad, and I tell you, he will be bad on some days, you must still love him, that's when you need a heart to forgive him, learning to leave many bad days behind you. It is through that forgiveness, you will show him the love inside of you and he will come to you for some of it each time, again and again. Do you know what I am saying?'

Claudia nodded in the positive.

'Then why do you ask me if marriage is a frightening thing? Those sticks are poking out, break some of them, let's not leave them behind, they make the fire last longer. Come on now, we must get down before sunset,' Gormai said, rising hurriedly to her feet. When they walked half way down the hill, Gormai picked up the conversation again. 'So what was I saying?'

'You said nothing, Gormai.'

'Girl, how can you turn such a long conversation into nothing?'

'Well, you said one must have a good strong heart to get married,' Claudia said stepping her way down carefully.

'Oh alright! Apart from a good heart you need to keep your will power going. But it won't be hard for you, I see that will to fight it out in you already, Claudia.'

'How do you know those things about me, the things I myself am not sure of?' Claudia chuckled, balancing the sack of dry leaves on her head.

'I fed you your first solid meal. I was the one to wean you to rice kanji. I gave you your first bath, oiling you and bathing you till you turned into a one year toddler. I washed your nappy cloths twice a day. You would wet nappy cloths in minutes.'

'Gormai!' She whimpered, embarrassed to hear Gormai raising her childhood antics, Gormai continued without paying a heed. 'If I didn't check on your nappy, your mother would either leave you wet or open. She was that careless. Never have I seen a timid woman like her in our Oroshim. A man needs a comforting lap during his bad times. Doesn't he? How will he build a home with a woman who fears even a petty struggle? Always teary, always fearful. Yes, times do threaten us sometimes but if you expect everything to be a mat full of hibiscus and mogra, why marry at all? Sit in your mother's lap, lifelong.'

'O Gormai, why do you always have to pick on Mother?'

'You may argue with me as much as you want to girl, but I have my opinion and I hold on to it.'

'And Mother has her own opinion and stories too. I don't know who to believe. I am hungry and in no mood to argue. Watch out Gormai, there's a slope. Slow! Slow!'

'O stop it girl. The slope is nothing new, we are hilly women, we don't slip that easily. All I am saying is, you don't think too hard. You'll make him a happy man. I just know you will, but we have to finalise the date soon. Before you know it, Lent will be here. You know that the church does not allow marriages during Lent.'

'We can always speak to Padkur, I see him every day, Gormai, it won't be such a big problem. New year is too early.'

'You must talk according to your age girl; Lent weddings don't happen in Oroshim. Only in rare circumstances like in the case of the girl being pregnant before marriage or something or if one of the parents are bedridden and they are in a hurry to get their children married. It happened only during Padre Raul's years, but that was very long back. He was a good priest, he gave more importance to people than rules.'

'Who got pregnant before marriage?'

'Quiet! Merde. Someone break this girl's mouth.'

'O Gormai, who can hear us in this deserted hill?'

'They better not. The village elders should never hear anyone talking these things openly. Anyway, leave everything else. Now listen, let's not delay the marriage. If it is delayed till Lent then we will have to have it in the scorching summer. No one likes sweaty weddings. New Year is the best time for a celebration,' Gormai said, grumbling along.

'I was looking forward to carnival,' Claudia sulked, remembering how she had requested Damiáno to be around in Oroshim this carnival so that he can enjoy the fanfare, she wanted to be there, especially to see him enjoy the carnival.

'You can enjoy carnival even after you are married. I played carnival putting my little ones outside on a bamboo mat. I would rush to the kitchen, the first hour of the morning, get the burnt black coating powder from the cooking vessels and rub it on everyone's face. My little ones would be fine with a feeder bottle filled with diluted sugar water.'

'Goodness Gormai! You were a rowdy.'

'Keep quiet you naughty girl, your father was just like me; fun loving and free. He would go missing all day during carnival, and my dear husband would roam the whole village to look for him, finally finding him making cocads, soaked in clay, under the gum tree. O my boy! How I miss you. May your soul rest in peace,' Gormai sighed, mumbling a prayer.

'Were you ever teased by a Portuguese lad, Gormai?' Claudia asked, trying to change the mourning mood.

'Hmm. Very often.'

'It must have been annoying, wasn't it, Gormai?'

'How can any girl get annoyed with such good looking, robust men? The Portuguese took us away from the dullness of life, and in exchange gave us our carnival, our feasts, our dances, the King Momo and so much fun and frolic. That's why we love them so much. How could we get annoyed with the attention from the handsome Portuguese men? At least I never did.' Gormai blushed, the wrinkle lines on her aged face clearly visible.

'Gormai a rowdy. Rowdy a rowdy.' Claudia teased her grandmother making up a little song. 'Your cigar puffs. Your boldness. Your admittance to like the Portuguese men and not hiding it. Your love story and your audacity to make that love story a success by asking God desperately to help, even though you knew how a love marriage would be looked down upon in our village. All of that rowdiness is what you are, Gormai, and I kind of like you for it. Just rubbing the black powder and leaving the children alone seems inadequate to represent such claim to rowdiness.'

Claudia loved to listen to old stories from Gormai, enjoying especially when she spoke of Father's childhood, knowing that Gormai always had something good to talk about Father. She loved Gormai all the more for it. Dropping the sack down in Gormai's backyard, Claudia washed her hands and feet by drawing out water from the big copper pot. 'Mother must be waiting. I'll go, Gormai,' Claudia rushed.

'Now don't leave that oil on your hair too long. Wash it before Sunday,' Gormai shouted from behind her.

After 1947, soon after India's Independence, all states had acceded to the union, but Goa still remained under the control of Portugal. Prime Minister Jawaharlal Nehru initiated dialogue with the Government of Portugal to release Goa and a few other minor Portuguese holdings to India, but the Salazar government did not agree to it. It was heard that after many diplomatic efforts failed, the Government of India initiated a highly strategic military plan.

On Sunday morning, before the sermon, the priest had a special announcement. On hearing news about the military troops entering Goa, the church had decided to announce a cautious alert in the community. It was announced during the first mass, Padkur said it would be done at every mass. Girls and women were asked not to be seen roaming freely. Padkur, Padre Jose, Sankistao, Luis Bakaar and most elders went out in the evening for house visits, warning people to be alert. They were concerned about the women and asked them to be indoors before the church bell chimed for Angelus, to step out only in broad daylight.

It saddened Claudia. Like her, Damiáno was attending the first mass. When the announcement was made, she turned to look around the pew where he sat. He had turned to look in her direction too. Their eyes met.

Despite the church warning, Claudia woke up while it was still dark. Now she had Father's watch. Every night she kept it near her pillow. It was 3:00 a.m. She rubbed her eyes. The house wasn't as dark as it used to be. When she rose to her feet, she saw a faint light near Father's cot.

'Who is that?' Mother called out when she heard the noise from Claudia's movement. It seemed like Mother had been awake the whole night, brooding, sobbing, worrying. She had found Mother doing that often, calling out to Father, in her sleep, often.

'It's me Mother,' Claudia said in a tender tone.

'Go to sleep, Claudia, it's not morning yet.'

'I don't think I can go back to sleep Mother; I feel fresh and wide awake. I'll just go out and see if I can find some coconuts lying around,' Claudia tried convincing Mother with a lie.

'Didn't you hear the announcement yesterday? Go to sleep,' Mother shouted sternly.

It was difficult to leave the house. To add to it she wore black. She, Jakin and Bula could now be easily recognised, even from a distance. She had to let go. Sooner or later she would have to stop meeting Damiáno. Very soon, Piedade Ferrao, the seafarer, was expected to arrive for a brief break from his job on the ship. Claudia went back to sleep, lying awake for some time, engaged in her thoughts.

Copper brass, arranged marriage

The feast tent outside the chapel was big, accommodating hundreds of feast attendees. Knowing well that she was being watched, Claudia sat nervously hovering closer to Gormai. Most folks were in their grand attire; men in suits and carrying crisp, perfumed handkerchiefs. Women wore special clothes; dresses in shimmering silk, good quality velvet, smooth Taffeta, all of them tailor-made well in advance, with the latest style; a bordering of zigzag lace, a lacy front piece, fancy wide collars, bordered pockets, front-buttoned, halter necked and a waist of plentiful gathers were some of the patterns one could spot on the feast dresses. They wore special gold ornaments too; beautiful flower necklaces, jewelled long earrings, chains with rose pendants and gold ornaments with intricate filigree work. Gormai wore a cotton sari; widows were expected to wear simple clothing, preferably dull shades of either black, dark blue, grey or a combination of those colours, folks called them blind colours. People respected widows who maintained a simple look and attitude; a sad countenance, hair twisted in a bun and no pony tails or braids, no earrings and no sandals. Being a widow, Gormai's overly simple look was acceptable in general but for a girl-seeing occasion, Claudia felt she was dressed down, with a simple daily wear black dress and low heeled sandals. She wished she had asked the tailor to put a frill or a fancy yoke or something to the dress but it was a mourning dress and it had to be stitched in a simple style. 'Be careful about my earrings,' Mother had repeatedly told her, though they were too tiny for such caution, but the pair of earrings was the only gold jewellery their family owned. Gormai had requested Karmin Timai to lend her gold bangles to Claudia, forcibly pushing them along Claudia's wrist. Claudia was not really comfortable with borrowed gold but Gormai had insisted that a bride-to-be had to show some gold on her.

For a few minutes Gormai glanced with narrowed eyes at the front rows, as though she was searching for someone. She then looked on either side of the pews, then at the back rows and back to the front row. 'There he is! In the second row. Do you see that grey suit?' Gormai said softly, bringing her mouth closer to Claudia's ear. The man in the grey suit turned to look behind; he too, like Gormai seemed to be looking around for someone. Gormai widened her eyes and her smile and waved subtly to the man, who acknowledged her back with an equally elated smile.

'Piedade Ferrao,' Gormai whispered to Claudia.

'The bald one?' Claudia whispered back with her eyes carrying a startled look in them.

'A little baldness is a sign of wisdom and growing fortune,' Gormai said. Claudia smiled, assuming that Gormai said it jokingly, but Gormai was serious it seemed. Having met Piedade on many occasions before, Gormai and Piedade were at ease on seeing each other, but Claudia was quite nervous, that's why she didn't smile back when he turned to smile at her, and then, she didn't expect him to be bald.

She was quick in noticing his suit pocket with a golden buckle pen. He kept pulling out his handkerchief to wipe his face; it was crisp and new, the cologne fragrance of which whiffed across every time he took the handkerchief out from his pant pocket. The suit itself looked brand new; three piece, softly padded in the shoulders and chest with neatly tailored lapels and a smart pocket square. The watch on his wrist was as dazzling as the gold pen in his pocket. Apart from the things on him, Claudia noticed that he was not much of a looker, yet the eyes of many female feast attendants were on him, even the priest acknowledged his presence by glancing often in his direction through his sermon.

'So Piedade is the hero of the feast tent,' Claudia said in her mind. As the mass ended, people were seen embracing one another in greeting. Soon, the Ferrao family began interacting with Gormai, then, Piedade Ferrao greeted Claudia with a customary 'happy feast' hug, which caused more nervousness in her than before. 'I hear you are waiting to visit the chapel fair, Claudia,' he commented in one of the dining sheds of the feast area. Claudia smiled but was caught with a bit of surprise with the information he had about her and immediately knew that Gormai must have spoken to him.

Piedade's family chose one of the food sheds in the corner which offered enough shade. The waiters served sausages and beef croquettes. Frothing beer bottles were brought to the table too. The Ferraos had formed a big group at the food shed; family, relatives and friends, all getting along like one big family. Through all that went on, most eyes were on Claudia, she could sense it. 'Servej?' Piedade looked at Claudia offering her the beer but she shook her head in the negative, with a polite smile. She never had beer before, though she was curious to try it; but secretly, not in public.

'She seems more interested in the feast fair,' one of Piedade's relatives commented. 'What else will a bride-to-be look for? Copper-brass of course and the fair is full of it,' Piedade's aunt commented as the rest of the family joined in to tease Claudia. That was not true, thought Claudia to herself; even if it was, she knew that Mother could not afford to buy copper brass, not even if she was marrying into a deserving family like Piedade's, even though she knew that the copper utensils, brass utensils and some gold accessories were needed for a girl to carry in her trousseau, as dowry.

'Cola then?' Piedade probed.

Claudia looked at Gormai and nodded in approval, when she saw Gormai give the go ahead with a nod of her head.

'After this we'll go to the fair,' Piedade said teasingly; the rest of his family looked at her teasingly too. The repeated joke was getting on her nerves now, she wished Gormai had not mentioned it to them.

The entire stretch of road at the chapel fair was crowded, with one end of the road selling fruits and vegetables while the other end had stalls brimming with copper brass. There were also stalls selling toys. The group halted at the inking stall; the machine created ink-etched drawings on the skin, usually a Jesus face or a cross permanently inked over the inner side of the hand or on the right thumb. 'Get a cross,' Gormai nudged, knowing it was high time for Claudia to get one like most catholic girls. Claudia wasn't interested; her gaze was more towards the artificial gold vendors.

The bridal dowry in Goa was not just the copper-brass; apart from the utensils, dowry meant a trousseau of good clothes, a cupboard, crockery, embroidered bed sheets, pillow covers, table cloth, sofa cloth, real gold jewellery, etc. Most girls also took along a little porcelain baby Jesus decorated with gold ornaments or a miniature Mother Mary adorned in similar fashion.

'Are they expecting copper brass and everything?' she softly questioned Gormai.

'We will find out.'

'Gormai, you know that we can't....'

'You are supposed to keep a polite tone girl. Behave your age, I told you before,' Gormai shushed her.

'The bald one is not as simple as you think, Gormai. His eyes are constantly on my body running all over me from head to toe with an expression that makes me embarrassed.'

'Funny girl you are Claudia, let him stare. You're a beautiful woman and he's a man after all,' Gormai chuckled softly. 'You just stay quiet and remain polite; just see how I handle everything,' she said with calm assurance.

When the Ferrao family walked back home from the fair, Gormai and Claudia walked along as well. Their family house was big, comfortable, almost every room furnished with expensive furniture and artefacts of brass and silver. The big teakwood table placed in the centre of the dining hall was full of an impressive lunch spread of savoury delicacies. Gormai knew how to command respect from others. She spoke a bit about Claudia's father, accompanied by lavish praises about what a great girl Claudia is, how intelligent she was and how hard working. Claudia wished she could nudge Gormai and tell her to stop it. 'Have mercy on the fatherless child, we can't afford any dowry,' she slipped in, in between her praise.

There was a sudden stunned silence at the lunch table, the Ferraos sympathising with Gormai and Claudia. It was the post lunch walk that made a big impression on Claudia; rows of mango trees, innumerable coconut trees overflowing with big, green coconuts, large jackfruits dangling on trees on one side, trees loaded with drumsticks, chickoos, bread fruit, papaya trees and bananas. There was abundance everywhere in the large stretch of land that the Ferraos owned. A few yards from the family house were a row of huts for the cattle; cows, ox, buffaloes and two giant fighter bulls. Pigs and fowls had separate fenced yards. Workers belonging to a local Kunbi tribe worked all around the property; they were the live-in servants of the Ferrao family.

Fresh dung cakes, salt fish and new hay lay drying in the sun. The backyard was full of pig slop, cattle fodder, cows in the huts, pigs in the sty, chickens shitting on the ground; all of it spread a peculiar, pungent odour. It was indeed the smell of abundance and prestige; that's how it was measured in the suburban areas, the village folk called it prosperity. The girl selected to settle in this family would be privileged, thought Claudia in her mind, the lavish abundance of the Ferraos overwhelming her greatly. This was what Father had dreamt for the three girls; Jakin, Bula and Claudia. The dream had failed him while he was alive; if ever there was an opportunity it could be revived it was now, Claudia was having this conversation in her mind.

On the way home, Gormai told Claudia that the Ferraos said they liked her, that they were willing to go ahead with the match even without dowry; they told Gormai that the priests and elders of Oroshim had given a good reference about Claudia. The news brought a strange thrill to her heart. Later that evening; sitting in front of the fire, while heating up water to bathe, Claudia was lost in thought of all the happenings of the day with the Ferraos. She understood well that this was a precious opportunity, and that she was one among the most fortunate girls around the suburbs. It would be the first time in many years that something good was about to happen for Claudia's family. Gormai told her that the Ferraos needed a little more time to decide if it was going to be a new year wedding or a summer wedding.

Claudia gazed at the fields and hills above. She would miss Oroshim so much. If it was going to be a New Year wedding; she would miss celebrating carnival in her village; the humour filled intruz skit, and also the villagers painting each other's faces and watching little boys throwing cocads. And then, she would have loved to watch Damiáno taking part in the village carnival for the first time ever; she smiled at the thought of it, just imagining his white skinned face coated with black coal.

Claudia also thought of the fun that went around with the village women. Seaman Mingu visiting Oroshim every year during carnival, when the village women looked forward to the carnival fun with Mingu. They ran around squeaking and laughing in the backyards, dodging around bushes, when Mingu chased them all, one by one and coated black coal over their cheeks, caressing their faces with his blackened, rough hands.

What else would Claudia miss in the village? Maybe the summer blossoming of the cashew trees, kokum trees and the black currants on the hills. Also, the sea bathers that flocked Oroshim each year during summer for their yearly health bath; men and women, taking shelter by the Oroshim beach for three days, cooking and sleeping under the open sky. The beachside dwelling summer visitors were friendly, humble and thankful; they narrated the stories of how their bodies developed immunity by immersing in sea water every year. Claudia liked spending time listening to the stories of these strangers, as she offered to bring them well water, local salt and some wood for their fire to cook food.

Through all the wisdom as well as the silliness that existed, she loved Oroshim, very much. Although it had stringent rules, yet if one followed those rules, the village elders as well as other folk eagerly came forward to bestow their love. They contributed generously during weddings. They took time to assist a sick neighbour. They were always happy when anything good happened to someone within the community. They had a way of altering names, more out of love, than convenience. Someone extremely tall was fondly called Lamttu. Francis was called Forsu. Lourenco was called Lorshu. Philomen became Philu. Caetano Caitu. Magdalena was called Magdu, and Martalian, Martu. Their neighbour Anton was called Bullock cart Anton because he owned a bullock cart. Araujo's family was referred to as Pershiakar because their grandfather once worked in the Persian Gulf. Vincent was called Motorkar since his father had once owned a motor car. Uncle Jose's family was called Lotterikar because their ancestors once won a lottery. D'Silva was called Kalsaonkar because he wore kalsao, the trousers, when most others wore a loin cloth.

As the thoughts flooded her mind, Claudia sighed at the possibility of leaving Oroshim. The fields, the hills and the mud paths of Oroshim had witnessed her maturing from a child to a young woman. All of her learning had come from Oroshim, mostly from accompanying Gormai—hillocks, wedding homes, child deliveries, vespers at church, crib visiting during Christmas, working at fields—Claudia was always there with Gormai. In the fields, among the labouring women, Claudia learnt many life's lessons; weeding the grass, adult gossip and jokes, songs with double meaning, taking rain checks, sowing, reaping, hand-crafting palm raincoats, the art of killing water snakes that crawled into the fields. Lessons she would never forget, ever.

The dark room

It was early December. When Claudia and her mother reached the mansion, she felt it was an unusual day at Paklin Bai's house. It didn't take much time to sense that the guests in her sitting room were not gathered for the normal partying like they did on previous weekends. It was strange also because the usual excitement on Paklin Bai's face was missing. Her loud, free laughter after a few glasses of wine was missing too. Mother was asked to attend to the guests. Arrange glasses for their drinks. Serve them croquettes. Pour tea to those who didn't want to drink hard liquor. Clean up the used cups, saucers and glasses.

Mother was occupied, so Claudia began with the kitchen chores; drawing well water, she filled the kitchen pots and moved to fill up the bath area. She didn't expect to bump into Damiáno. All the while she had been thinking he was in Daman. Both stood startled at each other's sudden unexpected appearance by the bathroom door, staring into each other's eyes, face to face. She still had the water pot balanced on her left hip. He was wrapped in his towel, just finished his bath. Claudia shifted her eyes from him, overwhelmed with a sudden shyness to find him without his clothes, just the bath towel wrapped around his waist. He appeared a bit stunned too with her sudden appearance right inside the mansion. For a few moments she just stood there nervously then moved as he signalled her to follow him. She gently lowered the water pot from her hip and looked around cautiously, making sure nobody saw her. She quietly followed him to climb the wooden staircase, unused for long, the stairs opening into a dimly ventilated passage that led into a narrow, windowless room. They called it the dark room.

Damiáno shut the wooden doors behind them, noiselessly.

'Minha querida!' He called out to her softly and reached out his hand to hold her.

'Bab.'

'We won't be here too long. You must have heard those people in the hall talk about the evacuation; the vessel has already come to take the people,' he said in a hurriedly hushed tone.

'Where are they sending us, Bab?'

'Not you dear. They are planning to send the Portuguese back.'

'Then what will happen to all of us, to the people who remain here in Goa?'

'If the Indian Government succeeds at this, you will remain here as an Indian.'

His words echoed faintly in the dark high-walled room.

He clasped her hands and released them from his, circling them instead around her waist, his touch sending a shiver all over her body. She had missed it for days; that soothing touch from him. His announcement was hard on her. And then he drew her into his arms, gasping, a bit breathless as he threaded his arms beneath her shoulders and hair.

'We may never meet again minha querida,' he whispered, nuzzling her cheek as she hugged him viciously and wanting to cry, her nostrils flared nervously at the sudden announcement. She drew closer to him and clung on tightly to his chest as though he was about to be pulled away from her any moment.

Damiáno wasn't familiar with the dark room. Claudia was the one who dusted and cleaned the room crammed with bundles of scrap paper, heaps of old books, large sacks of rice, damaged bicycles, unused big aluminium vessels, straw baskets filled with sea salt, containers of tamarind and bags of dried red chillies. Some afternoons, when the sunlight was at its brightest, she dusted and rearranged the things lying around unused. At other times of the day, the darkness was too heavy to see anything clearly in there.

This time though, when Claudia went inside the store room, it was nearing sunset. In the pitch darkness she could only feel Damiáno, and hear the sound of his heavy breathing when he touched her. His arm slid down, across her body, caressing her and then his fingers ran through her tangled hair as he gently cupped her face in his hands and kissed her.

In the dark, she failed to find any old blanket or bed sheet from the pile that she herself had arranged on the overhead wooden shelf. As she groped around, her hands felt a pile of folded jute bags which she gently pulled down and spread them carefully, turning the flooring into a bed of jute.

No one in the mansion would bother coming to that room, except when it needed cleaning or if something needed to be stored.

There in the forbidding blackness of the room he undressed her. In her mind she knew she had to flee from his presence, refuse to let him come closer. Perhaps she should have declined his invitation in the first place. Instead she found herself lying on her back in the dark, underneath him. Naked. As her desire got fierce, she was unable to speak, swallow or hear anything outside of her own thudding heartbeat.

The unexpected grief of a separation made them cling to each other with a passion that was desperately intense. Breathing hard with the anticipation of imminent excitement that swept through their bodies. Unashamed, urged by the fact that it could possibly be their last time together, they secured themselves in each other, casting aside every embarrassment, Damiáno and Claudia made love.

An indescribable feeling of bliss swept through her entire body. Not wanting to move away, she was in a bit of a tremor and lay wilfully gripped within his strong arms and muscular thighs. The thud of his heartbeat audible in her ears as a profound realisation that she wanted to stay in his arms for the rest of her life overpowered her mind.

The sound of their deep breathing stopped and an abrupt silence broke in. She groped in the dark to reach out and grab her dress. Opening the door silently, she rushed outside the dark room; checked her dress hooks and dusted the skirt of her dress.

At the kitchen, her hands and legs trembled in an uneasy nervousness as she regained her senses and recollected the few moments just spent with Damiáno in the dark room.

She was astounded at the way she had lost control, for those brief moments, forgetting everything and everyone else. Seemingly lost in another world with Damiáno.

The wrongness of those moments struck her with a sudden rudeness. Especially the thought of the recent meeting with the Ferraos. The fact that she would soon be married to someone else and not Damiáno surfacing with intensity, increasing the shame that swept over her heart. She hoped, again, that no one had seen them.

There was much more work to be finished at the mansion. She knew Mother would question her about it and so she wanted to hurry as fast as she could, and rushed to unclip dried clothes from the clothesline. In the yard, her gaze lifted to the upper window to find Damiáno engaged in discussion with the guests. He held a drink in his hand. His eyes met Claudia's and he smiled. Somehow, without realising it, she found herself unable to smile back.

The hurt that he would be leaving soon was much too strong. In her mind, she knew she could go on looking into his eyes, even from a distance, knowing she was deeply in love.

Mother returned from attending Paklin Bai's guests. Claudia was done with most of the kitchen work. Mother came to her and said, 'This time, if they ask for another round of tea and biscuits, you take it. The guests rewarded me with some cash. They will give you too. Go, at least be seen, and don't be shy,' Mother prodded.

'Mother, please. I am not going,' Claudia hesitated.

At sunset, Claudia and Mother left for the day. They observed neighbours huddled around the transistor radios to get news updates on the liberation movement. Men gathered together in small groups discussing the situation over bottles of cashew forte. News spread that hundreds of military tanks and armed military officials were stationed at the border across the hill. An uneasy panic was rapidly spreading across most parts of the village. Some said fish would not be available for some time with the fishermen afraid to go to sea. Some said prices of goods and food items will soar, causing shops to shut down. Typical to the usual village discussions, most news was baseless gossip; some were careless rumours, some of it, though, was true.

When the oil lamps in Claudia's home were put off at night, after Mother, Jakin and Bula fell asleep, Claudia was still awake. Thinking. She thought of Damiáno. She thought of Piedade Ferrao. She thought of Gormai and her instructions of keeping away from the white men. She thought of Mother. Sankistao. The church elders. Damiáno again. The community elders. Paklin Bai. Oroshim. The wedding. The more she tried thinking of other things, her thoughts kept going back to Damiáno. Her heart felt heavy thinking how painful it would be for her not to see him ever again. On the one hand, she felt the Portuguese should have never come to her village, while on the other hand, her heart was thankful that she had met Damiáno, to allow her the kind of pleasure that she would have never known existed. Thinking of him brought back the intimacy and passion of the dark room. She missed him with a longing that was almost unbearable and it got harder to stop thinking and let go of him. Her thoughts then drifted. A fear rose in her mind and grew gradually. She imagined Piedade or any of the elders finding out about what she did; then she imagined the intimate moments spent with Damiáno which quickly doused the fearful thoughts and sent a sensuous shiver through her body. The thoughts of pleasure and the pain went on until the early morning dawn.

Early the next morning, Claudia, her eyes filled with sleep and her head heavy, still got up to attend the first mass. Her mind was not really to pray as much as it was filled with a desire to see Damiáno. She hurriedly dressed and slipped out. At church, she kept looking, until the mass ended but Damiáno was not to be seen. Although it was a Portuguese mass there were very few of them for the early morning service. The church seemed half empty. The Priest reiterated the warnings and instructed people not to roam around, to remain indoors especially during night time, because of the uncertainty of the political situation as well as the strong military presence.

She finished the kitchen work at church and rushed to the big house, anxious to know if Paklin Bai's family was still there. As she neared the mansion she heard the big gates creak open and saw two men carrying luggage in their hand. They were piling bags inside Oliveira Bab's vehicle which was parked near the wall outside the gate. Claudia entered shutting the gate partially as the men walked back, when Oliveira Bab stepped out holding his briefcase.

'Claudia!' he called out, his expression telling her that he did not expect her to show up, 'As you must be knowing, we are about to leave, he said, and began to secure the mansion gate with a big lock and a chain, with the help of his companions. She nodded.

'Where is Bab, Damiáno Bab?' she asked, when she knew she should have been asking for Paklin Bai. 'They have already left, Claudia,' Oliveira Bab answered and thinking she was looking for Damiáno to ask for money, he pulled out some and placed it in Claudia's hand.

'Take care of yourself, Claudia,' Oliveira Bab told her, getting into his vehicle in a rush. The vehicle sped, away from the big gate, past the tall pine and banyan trees, leaving a trail of dust behind. Claudia stood staring until the vehicle disappeared from her sight. She peeped inside through the gap between the big gates. Stared at the mansion and its surroundings; the garden plants needed watering. Pine cones and dry leaves had scattered around, the yard had to be swept. The copper pot, tied to its coir rope, rested idly over the water well. The big washing stone in one side of the yard lay dry, where she breathed into his clothes before rubbing them hard against the stone to clean every speck of dirt and sweat mark. The balcao, where Damiáno often sat to read his books was empty. In the frontyard was the Atlas cycle on which they both explored many bushes and tambdimati paths to get away from everyone around. She continued to peep into the mansion for long. She had worked there for too long to be able to take in such an abrupt end of it all. The pain surfaced and welled up her eyes. Controlling her longing to cry out loud, Claudia walked back home with deep sadness, to tell Mother that they don't have to work anymore at the big house, that Paklin Bai and her family had left, for good.

Seeing Damiáno

Except for the military presence and the latest buzz of rising political tension between the Portuguese and the Indians, things were as usual at this time of the year in Oroshim. It was mid December. Young boys engaged themselves in the making of a Christmas crib. They soaked wheat in advance to sprout in order to give a more authentic and natural look to the manger. Except for the grass, everything else was artificial. Mary, Joseph and infant Jesus along with shepherds, a few sheep, angels and other farm animals as well as the three wise men were ready to be placed around the crib to display the nativity scene; all clay art objects. With skilful efforts, the boys busied themselves to hand-craft the manger of bamboo sticks and straw.

Women were engaged in the preparation of Christmas sweets, especially the traditional sweet puff filling. Sesame seeds, cardamom, poppy seeds, good quality semolina; a lot went into making that filling. The younger kids though, mainly boys, were not as much focussed over Christmas preparations as they were in gathering around the borom trees to collect the seasonal sweet sour berries. Some climbed the tree and shook its branches forcefully. Some waited underneath to gather the fallen berries until they collected enough to divide the berries in equal portions among each one present.

Paklin Bai had just left Oroshim for good and the change was too sudden and hard on Claudia. After a long time, she had some free time at hand. When she saw the boys picking berries, she decided to join them too. They had also lit up a bonfire which would keep her warm from the chill. The boys were happy to give her a handful of berries which she dumped in the flare of her skirt, popping them one by one in her mouth, occasionally chewing a bad berry and making funny faces each time her tongue got its rotten taste. The little boys enjoyed her look and laughed. They engaged Claudia with many neighbourhood stories, things like which borom tree was the best. Old, childless Pishi Timai and her equally ageing husband's backyard gave the juiciest and the sweetest of boroms, they told her, the reason why they sneaked out to that tree. Pishi Timai's husband was a hot tempered man who chased the naughty boys with his sharp iron axe. The boys laughed much as they narrated to Claudia how Pishi Timai yelled out to her husband to help her every time the pelted stones fell on her roof tiled house 'Jaki Santan, they are back to break our house.' The boys, never having attended any school, and with plenty of idle time, engaged themselves in ragging people who were easy to annoy; the only disciplined time they spent was during catechism at church, once a week. After finishing her share of berries, Claudia left to go about her daily chores, promising to join the little boys again on the condition that they will not trouble Pishi and her husband.

For Claudia, the time with the kids was a good distraction, at a time when she missed Damiáno much.

The days went by with unusual constance. Nothing seemed to change. The village folk continued anxiously tuning in to their transistors to get the latest update on the liberation movement. The educated ones scoured the newspaper. Claudia hastened to get to work at the church kitchen. She realised that the news had been constant for a while; attempts of Goa being set free from the Portuguese rule, the presence of armed forces, Portuguese resistance, India and the Indian Government, Portuguese India and the government in Portugal, Jawaharlal Nehru and António de Oliveira Salazar. It was the only news that made repeated rounds.

After hanging out the priests' cassocks on the drying line, Claudia went upstairs, where Sankistao was cutting vegetables. 'So I heard some good news, I wanted to hear it directly from you,' Sankistao exclaimed with a curious smile on his face.

'Gormai told you?'

'I overheard when she spoke about it to Padkur. And you better hurry and say yes to an early wedding, girl. There are a dozen girls waiting to grab Piedade, there is none more eligible than him among the good bachelors, you know it. Our ancestors would say that one needs seven pairs of slippers to have one wedding. Look at you! It took your Gormai only one pair of slippers,' he teased.

'Not even one, Gormai came there barefooted; she gets cramps with slippers and ends up losing one every time she wears footwear.'

'See, what did I say? Not even one pair of slippers.' Sankistao laughed and they both enjoyed that little joke. Though, at that moment, Claudia had much on her mind. 'Did you hear that the fishermen are not going to catch fish, fearing the war?' she asked.

'You can never tell how the situation will turn out, girl.'

'What's the latest news you heard on your transistor, Sankistao. Will they allow the Portuguese families who left to come back?'

'Claudia, you are going to be a bride soon. It's high time you stopped worrying about the war or the Portuguese. Wars will start and wars will cease.'

'Is there a chance for them to return, Sankistao? That's all I asked.'

'So he is giving you false hopes that the families will return. Is that why he came here? It's a good thing I had the presence of mind to tell him you are not here. The decision you take now is very crucial for you and your household, I am telling you Claudia. I wouldn't let him come in to see you, no matter how much he tried convincing me. You see, I am not usually the kind to say no to people, but I had to.'

'Who?'

'Damiáno Bab.'

'Damiáno Bab came here?' Her nostrils flared as she asked. Sankistao nodded.

'Look Claudia, I am a faithful servant of this church. I will not let anyone ruin the lives of our village girls. I wouldn't let him in, no matter how much he tried convincing me, so he left.'

‘Why didn’t you…?’ Claudia chose to run downstairs without wasting time to argue. She enquired with the cemetery keeper who was sitting at the gate. Calmly, the cemetery keeper’s curious eyes studied Claudia before he pointed his finger towards the church entrance. She followed his direction. Dipping her fingers in the holy water outside the entrance, as was customary to do before one entered the church; Claudia barged in while still applying a sign of the cross over her forehead. There he was kneeling down. His hands clasped. The church was empty inside. Except for him.

Quickly she knelt next to him. ‘I thought you were gone, Bab,’ she whispered, her heart pounding faster.

‘I came to meet you, Claudia.’

‘It’s not good to talk here, Bab. Let’s go to the cemetery. Follow me.’ She rose to her feet and moved out quickly. The cemetery was deserted when Claudia entered. A warmish breeze blew from the palms and plants. Bougainvilleas, pink roses, red roses, white roses, sweet fragrant mogras and hibiscus flowers bloomed in the graveyard; most of them planted by those who had lost their loved ones. The palm trees were planted by the church authorities. Damiáno entered behind her and they stood facing each other, under the shade of the big neem tree.

‘I have tipped the cemetery caretaker. He is not going to let anyone in; he has locked the gate from outside.’ Damiáno said trying to calm her nervousness.

‘He is not supposed to do that, Bab.’

‘It’s okay my dear,’ he said, holding her hands in his. ‘But we must hurry. Listen minha querida, we thought our mansion was very Portuguese and can be easily found in the middle of the small mud houses in Oroshim. You know Papa holds an important position in the government. Mamma was afraid, so we had to take precautions to be safe and decided to shift temporarily. We told everyone we are off to Portugal, while we actually moved in with my aunt, who stays in a remote village. It was hard to see Mamma panic.'

'So you are not leaving.'

'We are Claudia, that's why I came all the way. Just to ...'

'Bab, there is not much privacy here.' She swallowed hard.

'I know. Something inside me was too restless, and I was getting this feeling that maybe it's you, I mean all this restlessness could be because you are here. You understand what I mean. Anyway, I came to ask you if you would come with me to Portugal?' he said it abruptly, with an anxious, expectant look.

His question stunned her. She stared at him, speechless. The nervousness of their presence near the church troubled her. The priests were at the church itself. Her meeting with Damiáno would become a big issue, if anyone got the slightest hint about it.

'I tried to convince my parents that Mamma really needs you as she settles back in Portugal. It was all I could think of to take you along with me ....' he said, and added reluctantly, '... as a domestic servant.'

Overwhelmed by the moment, Claudia didn't know how to react. On the one hand, she was really touched to know that he had come back to take her along, while on the other hand, she was confused at his request. It was too quick and too hard. Absolutely unexpected.

'My dear, it will all be fine once we reach Portugal.'

'Mother won't let me go, Bab. Not just Mother, Bab it's not safe for you to talk to me here. And then ...'

'I promise to take very good care of you,' he said, trying to reassure her.

The noise of the clanging gate jolted them to alertness; the cemetery keeper indicating them to come out. Claudia moved closer to Damiáno, wanting to say so much when she looked into his eyes. 'Before dawn, I will be waiting at the gum tree. If I find you waiting for me, we will leave for Tia Lourdes' house from there,' he said in a rush of words.

'Bab ...'

'But,' Damiáno halted before he went on to say, 'if at all I don't see you there, this will be that goodbye, minha querida.' He stroked her cheek with the back of his fingers and left the cemetery. After a minute, Claudia stepped outside, the cemetery keeper watching her intently. She didn't want to meet his gaze, though his inquisitive stare made it hard to ignore. Promising him more money from her side, Claudia headed to the church kitchen, requesting the cemetery keeper to let no one know about what had happened.

'Don't worry. I won't tell anyone,' he muttered.

Plates with bits of left over fried eggs and crumbs of hard crusted bread were still at the table. The priests were just gone; Claudia heaved a sigh before clearing the table. She wasn't sure if Sankistao had told the priests anything about her, though she prayed that he hadn't. Silently, Claudia finished her work at the church kitchen, her mind clogged with thoughts concerning Damiáno. He was leaving, and, this could be that goodbye as Damiáno had said, but, if she met him at the gum tree before dawn, she could spend a lifetime with him, in Portugal.

'I am leaving, Sankistao,' she announced, still lost in her own thoughts.

'You are not upset with me, are you? Claudia, you are like a daughter to me, I said this before. When I see you, I don't miss being with my daughter. You must know that I really wish you well.'

'I will pray that your daughter visits you someday, Sankistao. Someday she will, I get a feeling about it.'

'I wait for that day Claudia.'

'But ... we must realise Sankistao, that if a person goes away, that person could be your daughter or anyone, we should not think that she went because she does not care. The truth is, she does care. Hmm?' She nodded questioningly. With that nervous muttering from her, Sankistao's gaze grew suspicious. His lean body curled up and the wrinkles on his forehead loosened to a frown, jaw drooped, he stared at her in confused silence.

'I am leaving, Sankistao,' she told him again, this time rushing down without waiting a moment. As she reached the last step of the stairs, something made her halt; when she looked back, she saw him still staring in her direction. He had the same expression; jaw drooping, squint-eyed, disoriented posture. 'Whatever you do, do it wisely.' he said, with a strange nostril-flared smile.

That evening, hoping to find some fish, Claudia visited the fishermen's huts before sunset. She wanted to cook dinner that night, but she found no fish with the fishermen remaining indoors in their palm leaf huts, probably afraid to wander out to cast their nets, after the rumour buzz spread panic. Claudia managed to get some dried fish from their stored stock. For dinner, she made dry fish curry and rice, after which, she left for the bazaar and bought two bunches of dried tobacco leaves. Plucking some berry leaves on her way back from the bazaar, she headed straight to Gormai's house to find her at the balcao, sipping black tea.

'Do you want to have tea?' Gormai asked her.

'No. I will go home and have it. I went out to get this for you. Here, tobacco leaves for your cigar; I also plucked a few big sized berry leaves.'

'When did I tell you to bring this?'

'O Gormai! You didn't hear that the fishermen are not going to the sea? They are afraid of getting bombed at sea, it seems. Who knows, the bazaar may be closed for days. I bought this with my own money; you don't have to pay for it.'

'Does your Mother know you spent this money on me?' Gormai asked, not knowing how to react to the touching gesture from her young granddaughter.

'The money is from my earning.'

'Child, I'll miss you much after you are gone. But go you must. Old grandmother's eyes have longed to see you in your white veil standing next to Ferrao. Don't forget, he called you to visit the fair again. Huh? God bless the boy! We should go back to the fair, once the situation calms a little. Should we?'

'Do you think the fair is still there?'

'I think so. Usually, they don't clear it before two weeks after the feast.'

'You finish your tea, Gormai. I must go now.'

'Wait. Fold your hands, let me bless you. There are not many young girls out there who get tobacco for an old woman. You are a good girl. Go, be blessed, grow big.' It was a typical way an elder blessed younger folks, that Gormai blessed Claudia with. The 'Grow Big' didn't necessarily mean in height, but a metaphor for prosperity.

'I am not all that good, Gormai. I must confess I have done some bad things.' Claudia said wanting to tell it all, though a kind of fear held her back.

'Well, what did you do?' Gormai questioned promptly, with a curious, puzzled look.

That question got Claudia wondering how much she could reveal to Gormai, as she tried to camouflage her thoughts with a nervous laugh which eased the sudden anxiousness on Gormai's face. 'First of all I got fish once from the fishermen, and told them your name. I lied to them that you asked for it to take it to the priests.'

'Oh! And they must have given you the best fish they could, isn't it? I have played that trick many a times. It works. Just say it's for the priests and get some good fish home, or else they usually keep smelly and stale fish to give away,' Gormai laughed, amused with herself.

'You are a rowdy. I always told you that,' her eyes moistened as she teased her Gormai.

'And you are a lot like me; see how you learnt my tricks.'

In that moment of unreserved bonding, Claudia wished she could express everything to Gormai. She wasn't this close with anyone else. No one else was as concerned about her well being as Gormai. She was wise. Experienced. Caring. Claudia ached to bare her heart out, as the burden of her thoughts and emotions seemed to burst inside her head. At that moment, she knew, if she uttered even one more word to Gormai, she would break down. So she remained silent. She realised, how much it meant to Gormai to see Claudia married to Piedade Ferrao. It would be a risky thing for Claudia to even hint about Damiáno. Who knows maybe Gormai would gather the entire village to stop Claudia from leaving and make sure the wedding between Claudia and Ferrao didn't fail in any way.

When she reached home Mother instructed her to keep an eye on the bathing water fire. 'Claudia, let Jakin have a bath first,' Mother said.

'Alright Mother.' She agreed to let Jakin go for her bath first, just like Mother instructed. A little while later, Jakin came with a big bundle of dried leaves for the fire and when she saw Claudia sitting in front of the fireplace, she said 'Go for your bath, Claudia,'

'You go first Jakin. Mother complains that we always make you go last for bath.'

'It's alright, I am the eldest. Father expected me to take care of you both. When you were a baby, I was the one to get a shouting, if you ever fell.'

Jakin's response surprised Claudia, especially when she pulled a wooden stool to sit beside her. It had never happened that the sisters had discussed anything of the past or about Father before. Why now? Claudia wondered. She had to be alert to make sure her plan to go with Damiáno did not reach Jakin's ears.

'Do you know that Father had a cycle?' Jakin asked. 'We were not poor then,' she added.

'I remember the red cycle!'

'Before the red, he owned another one, a very good one. He would take all three of us on a ride, taking turns with each of us. He cheated me and Bula a little to give you a longer ride. If we got one ride, you would get three.'

'So I was his favourite?'

'We all were, until a few years back. He pampered you more because you were born twelve years after us. You were the baby of the house. But you will be surprised, he was initially disappointed, he had expected Mother to give birth to a boy and you came instead. You won him over and around the time you were getting to be a one-year-old, he began telling everybody what a great little girl you were. He didn't change his mind until he died, don't you think so Claudia?'

'Well.'

'My rice flour, Father would call you. And you really were a pretty baby. Of course, you are even better now.'

'I remember the rice flour thing,' Claudia laughed softly, still wondering what was going on in Jakin's mind.

'You are special Claudia. Everybody likes you. I notice that even those who don't like us, still like you. And Gormai, she would not even come home a few years back. Even the church had stopped giving us any attention. But you changed it all. Padkur. Sankistao. Gormai. Paklin Bai. Damiáno Bab. Father.' One name on Jakin's list surprised Claudia even more, her thoughts immediately drifting towards Damiáno.

'You know Claudia, I can never forget the look in his eyes when he looked at you.'

'Damiáno?'

'Not Damiáno Bab. I am talking about Father.' Jakin corrected, but looked strangely at her sister, that awkward moment making Claudia's face flush.

'Do you know what the look in his eyes said, Claudia?'

'What?'

'Don't do what Jakin and Bula did.'

'Maybe.'

'Never forget that when Father looked at you, he saw a last hope. I can't tell you how angry I am at myself for letting him down.'

Claudia watched Jakin wipe her tears with the duster that lay near the water pot. 'Why a married man?' Claudia broke the silence, though she knew it was an uncomfortable question to answer, but it had just slipped from her mouth.

Jakin breathed in deep, her answer was calm. 'He didn't tell me he was married until his wife found out about us. The wife complained to the church authorities. He was a toddy tapper who visited Oroshim occasionally. No one really knew him well. Mother pleaded with the priests to hush the matter and to pardon the mistake but he said a sin like that had to be highlighted so that other parents in the village would remember to discipline their daughters.'

'And they were so nasty that they treated Bula just like you.'

'Bula was pregnant.'

'Bula what? No one ever told me about it. What happened to her baby then?'

'Claudia, you are not a little girl anymore, you know what girls in Oroshim did if they got pregnant before marriage?'

'What did they do? I don't know of anyone who ...'

'It was aborted.'

'Poor Bula,' Claudia sighed.

'It was her choice. I had warned her. But you know Bula, she wanted it all. How can anyone trust a man who offers a young girl beer in his wife's absence?'

'Where would his wife be?'

'They would be alone when his wife left for the daily bazaar trip. One day when she returned home and saw them together in a way she didn't expect, she raised her voice, loud enough to gather the village folks around their house. The man escaped, but Bula had to take the brunt of the village anger.'

Jakin cleared her throat and tried to change the talk. 'But things were not always stressful at home. We were so playful and free with each other before all the wrong things happened. Claudia, do you remember Father playing marbles with you?'

'No.'

'Well. You loved marbles. Gormai would yell if she saw a marble in your hand because you would pop it into your mouth. In her absence, Father would give you a handful of them and play with you. If he had to go out, he would tell me to keep an eye on you. One day I got too involved in playing and Father reached just as you swallowed a little blue marble. You should have seen the way he scolded me. Badly. You cried. I cried. Mother cried.'

'Obviously! And then?'

'Mother found it the next day in your stools. It was not too big a marble.'

The two girls shared an unexpected laughter, though the discussion with Jakin made Claudia more and more suspicious. By any chance did she suspect something?

'Jakin, Claudia, come inside. Close the doors now, it's getting dark. Mosquitoes are coming in,' Mother called out to them from inside.

After the night meal of rice and dry fish curry, when the kerosene lamps were put off, Claudia felt heavy. It could be her last night in Oroshim. The big cloth bag she had packed that afternoon, lay hidden under Father's cot; two changes of clothes, some undergarments, a comb, hair oil and face powder was all she had packed. The clothes in the bag were four tailored knickers, two petticoats, three cotton house dresses and two church dresses.

Claudia lay awake, anxiously. Eloping to another country wasn't an easy decision. A life outside of Oroshim was difficult to imagine. She may not be able to see the people that meant so much to her; Mother, Jakin, Bula, Gormai, Sankistao, the neighbours, the field wosrkers and all the people she had grown up with. Although it was a hard decision, her desire for Damiáno overpowered everything else. There was not a person or place or anything that could take the place of Damiáno, she felt.

As the fierce, conflicting thoughts swelled up in her mind, she realised that there was something about Oroshim that would live with her forever. She sighed and shook her legs restlessly, biting her lip trying hard to release the stress. As her mind continued to struggle, a strong passion rose from inside, when she thought of Damiáno. Choosing to live without Damiáno was like choosing to live without a part of herself, nothing around her would make sense, she thought. She just knew how badly she wanted to spend the rest of her life loving Damiáno, and though tough, it was her decision, at the moment. It was the most overpowering thought running in her mind, over and over again.

The Portuguese are leaving

From a distance Claudia could see a small flicker of light in the dark. It could be anybody; a man smoking his beedi, a military man on duty, a local, or even a firefly. With a torch of dried palm leaves in one hand and her bag of essentials in the other, Claudia halted for a moment.

As she watched, the light sprang high up, went down, and in a moment, disappeared into the night air. Firefly! Claudia exclaimed absentmindedly and continued to walk. The insects were common around the bunds and fields. At times, the firefly's light would be the only visible light in the dark field paths.

After having walked halfway from home, she could sense someone coming behind her. This time it wasn't a light. It was the sound of footsteps. In Oroshim, there was a strong superstition that one should not turn behind to look, when out on an important task. Of course the escape was an important task, a sensitive one too. The footsteps got louder while the thought of the ill effects of turning back was still on her mind.

It could be someone from home, in which case she'd have to run, though she was sure that Mother, Bula and Jakin were fast asleep when she left. She slowed down and the footsteps behind her slowed down too. She hurried her steps and the footsteps behind seemed to hurry as well. Someone was following. Drawing a hard breath through her nostrils, she walked towards the gum tree. She should have run, instead, she turned to look back.

'Claudia!'

'Bula go! Is that you? Bula.'

'It's me Jakin.'

'Why are you following me? Go!' Claudia shouted at her, in a loud and irritated voice.

'Shh! Talk softly. You'll get into trouble if anyone hears us.'

'Jakin go back. You can't stop me.'

'Where are you going?'

'To Portugal. With Damiáno. I want to be with him.'

'What? No Claudia. You're making a big mistake because you're messing up the chance to marry Piedade. Do you realise that? Not just that, this can make you lose all the love our village elders and the community has for you. You will have no respect or hope left, unless you want to end up like me and Bula.' As Jakin spoke, the sudden noise of a speeding vehicle interrupted them. It stopped near the ruins. Jakin instinctively grabbed Claudia's wrist tightly. 'Claudia!' A husky voice echoed strong. The moment Claudia heard the voice, she dropped the fire torch from her hand and wrestled hard to free her hand from Jakin's tough grip.

'Let me go, Jakin. Please,' she cried out, unable to break free from her older sister's strong grasp.

'Claudia, I plead with you, if coming back is the slightest option in your mind, please stop yourself right now.'

'Just let me go,' Claudia repeated, sternly.

The fire from the fire torch spread wider on the ground as the argument went on; Jakin desperately pleading with Claudia not to go, while Claudia shaking her wrist adamantly to free herself from Jakin. Seeing her persistence, Jakin released her sister's hand, with a sniffing noise and exclaimed, 'Go!'

Claudia saw that she was trying hard to hold back crying aloud. Claudia stood still, breathing hard, just like Jakin, both caught in a mix of emotions: anger, grief, sisterly love or something else that wasn't expressed ever.

After a few moments, Claudia ran fast towards Damiáno. Inside the vehicle, there was a man sitting in the front seat, Damiáno was at the driver's seat. And she had thought it would be a private ride for her and Damiáno alone. Nobody spoke in the vehicle for a while. Damiáno looked tense. After a few minutes of drive, Claudia learnt that he had to pick up more people in his vehicle.

Sitting in the back seat, Claudia watched the familiar sights of her dear village as the vehicle sped along its now seemingly eerie paths. It was hard to think that the bunds, coconut palms and hills, grazing cattle and all the natural surroundings that beautified Oroshim would be overpowered by a military presence. Covering herself in Mother's cotton ole, Claudia wondered if the war would change Oroshim's natural beauty. Would the bombing destroy the thatched huts? What about the haystacks and fields? The thought of a possible destruction worried her. 'But will that help in bringing about a change in the way the locals looked at life? Will the elders stop being judgmental and stop imposing those hard rules, if they were told that Oroshim was going to be wiped out overnight in the war?' She doubted it. She had sensed that the minds of the local folk were not so easy to change, especially the elders, they had bound the community with their rules, setting their own parameters and conditions to live in the village.

'We are out of Oroshim,' Damiáno announced, turning for a brief second towards Claudia.

'Where are we going now, Bab?'

'Tia Lourdes' house. She and Uncle Ronald live in a big house in Raitura. It's far from here.'

'They *lived* in a big house. Not anymore. It's over for all of us, or so it seems.' The man in the front seat, cribbing in anger, spoke Portuguese.

After driving a distance, Damiáno slowed down to inspect the road and the surroundings, before he stopped the vehicle. Claudia watched curiously. Probably the man would get off and leave them both alone. She longed to hear Damiáno say, like he often did, *Dá-me um beijo*, give me a kiss. As the car halted, the other Portuguese man got down from the vehicle, walking swiftly towards the lane. Claudia moved closer towards Damiáno's back. He turned around, with his hands resting on the steering, and asked her to push up and make space for a family who, she understood, was accompanying them. For a brief moment Damiáno and Claudia were alone in the vehicle waiting for the family to join them; she learnt that the man had got off to bring the family to the vehicle.

Damiáno turned back, Claudia inched closer, he touched her face, his sturdy fingers stroking softly across her cold cheek. Half his attention was towards the lane, as he told her, 'If the situation does not permit me to talk to you, through the journey or anytime, you shouldn't feel lonely. Ask for help if you must. Mamma will be around, ask her for things. And remember, minha querida, no one gets a hint about anything between us. Alright?'

Claudia nodded, her gaze pleading, desperately trying to get more attention from him.

The Portuguese man got back into the car after ushering a family of three. Claudia pushed herself towards the corner of the back seat. The head of the family was introduced to her as a professor. On and off there were discussions in Portuguese. The Portuguese soldiers were out to fight, hundreds of them. They discussed. Claudia's head ached, having been awake all night.

The professor and his wife seemed tense, but what surprised Claudia more was that, in spite of the difficulty of the situation that confronted them, the Portuguese folks who had just joined them seemed quite curious about Claudia and wanted to know what a non-European was doing among them. The professor's wife kept glancing at Claudia with an intensely questioning look. It was obvious, Claudia's appearance and skin colour could reveal a lot and even arouse curiosity.

For one, she certainly didn't look Portuguese, but on the other hand, she didn't look like a typical housemaid. Claudia had always carried herself gracefully and maintained confident expressions with an air of sophistication that could not be assigned to her profession as a maid.

The couple in the vehicle whispered closely to each other in Portuguese, casting glances all the time in her direction.

Claudia knew they were talking about her, it made her more anxious than she already was. There was so much that had already brought in anxiety and fearfulness.

'Are you Portuguese, Senhorita?' The man questioned her in native Portuguese with a raised eyebrow.

'No,' Claudia answered, smiling and feeling humbled to be even considered to be Portuguese.

'Then she must be with you?' The man excitedly questioned the other man in the vehicle with half confidence in his voice, almost as though he was wishing he was correct.

'No she's not with me,' the man replied, curtly.

'Claudia is with me.' Damiáno's confident voice emerged and everyone went silent. In hushed tones, they all spoke to Damiáno and discussed who she was. When Damiáno announced that Claudia works in their house and would be travelling with them to Portugal, the atmosphere in the vehicle became somewhat awkward.

By turns, everyone in the vehicle began to give her inquisitive looks, all the while continuing to smile, a bit more generously than before. It made Claudia feel absolutely uncomfortable. She wished they had not asked who she was. She could sense the awkwardness on Damiáno too and that bothered her more. It was important to her that Damiáno's reputation was not tarnished in anyway. She never wished for him to face unpleasant situations ever, least of all, because of her. Raw emotions rose along with a lump in her throat. She felt a longing to get out of the vehicle and cry out loudly. She wanted to desperately get rid of the housemaid tag that got associated with her. It was certainly not what she would have ever wanted to be known as, while growing up. She would have loved to study and work in a respectable profession, like a seamstress or maybe even a nurse, anything but not branded as a housemaid. As the hurt rose, a feeling of consolation slowly overpowered her mind. This was what destiny had chosen her to be, a servant girl. The thought consoled her, if she wasn't a housemaid she would not have met Damiáno—her lover, her happiness, the man she wanted to spend the rest of her life with.

The dialogue between her and Jakin repeated itself in her head. She couldn't help thinking of the way Jakin had caught her leaving the house, and of the way they both argued bitterly near the gum tree.

Damiáno took diversions, speeding by the rough streets, every time he sensed the presence of military officials or vehicles. He drove through bunds and muddy bylanes; even barren fields. The vehicle gave some trouble on the way, it was expected with the way Damiáno had been driving, through fields, rubble and stones, in order to find short cuts so that no one would stop them. They were stopped twice, well almost twice, the first stop fortunately was by two Portuguese soldiers; a little questioning and Damiáno was allowed to move on. The second stop was by a group of officials in their khaki attire, Damiáno defied them, speeding away in spite of the uneven narrow lanes.

Claudia was happy to see Paklin Bai again, even more thrilled to get a warm hug from her. 'Claudia! I thought you would not come, happy you joined us, dear.' Claudia could tell she was happy to see Claudia again as well. Inside Tia Lourdes' house, morose faces greeted her; an anxiety filled asylum, the house seemed to her. The sun was already out, when another couple joined them. A little later, some more panicked faces entered the scene. News was going around that the Portuguese soldiers were spotted in battle clothing, marching into the Basilica. Soldiers praying for help it seemed like.

Paklin Bai, Tia Lourdes and the other ladies got along talking. They cried a little; mouthing hateful words in Portuguese towards their enemy. None seemed to have the appetite to eat, most of them drinking plain tea. Claudia felt hungry but nobody was talking of food. As more people joined in, more news filled the house along with more panic and tears. The outcome of the attack was still unpredictable. Many among the gathered folks were Portuguese government officials holding esteemed positions, just like Oliveira Bab.

'This bag is important. Be careful with it. I'll tell you when I need it,' Paklin Bai said softly to Claudia. Claudia nodded and peeped slowly to see what was inside the bag: two wine bottles clumsily wrapped around with a newspaper. Damiáno, when spotted, was occupied in accommodating the families and folks he brought in his vehicle. Paklin Bai was busy talking with the other ladies. Tia Lourdes along with the professor's wife and a few others went out to the backyard to pluck some fruits. Papaya trees, borom trees, banana saplings, guava trees as well as a tree of custard apples were in Tia Lourdes' backyard. They plucked two large semi-ripe papayas and some fully ripe custard apples and served at the table. Some ate; the rest simply didn't bother, with most of them eager to leave for the airport to get to their own country, none of them sure though of when it would happen.

News spread that the Indian contingent was moving through minefields and roadblocks, but the one that caused a stir among the public was the buzz that the Portuguese forces were about to withdraw. It was disturbing news that the bridges were being destroyed; Borim Bridge, Quepem, the Banastari Bridge as well as roadways and sea routes. How could they leave for Portugal if the Bridges were destroyed, how would they get to the airport? The ladies engaged in a deep discussion and were much saddened when the news of the radio station Emissora de Goa being bombed came. After all, the radio station was much loved. It was a thing to which family members partied and waltzed to. It was Emissora de Goa which transmitted their favourite songs.

The Portuguese in Tia Lourdes' house discussed nothing but the war. News was brought in about the highly strategic military plan of the Indian government called 'Operation Vijay' to free the Portuguese colonies in India, which was enforced on 11th December 1961 when Indian armed forces crossed the border into Goa. Immediately, on the 12th December 1961, the land routes connecting Goa and the rest of India were blocked for civilian movement and only army personnel and their vehicles were allowed to move. Operation Vijay was set up with everything prepared for an aggressive military attack on the 18th of December 1961 for which the Army, Navy and Air Force participated. At 6:30 a.m. the Operation began with the Indian Air Force planes bombarding the radio station at Bambolim and the airport at Dabolim. Simultaneously, Indian Navy ships were moved into position outside the Marmagao port. It was believed that there was sustained land, sea and air strikes for more than thirty six hours.

This must be a big war, thought Claudia; her mind drifting to Sankistao. He was right after all. A war can break out anywhere, Love and war can happen anywhere, he had once told her. The war was happening; love too had happened. Why else would she be here, hiding under a Portuguese dominated roof?

A multitude of thoughts, each accompanied with different emotions ran through her mind as she pondered over the situation. Part of her was overjoyed for what was happening; that she would be in Portugal, living in the same house as Damiáno, for the rest of her life. That thought was immediately accompanied with the worry of living as a servant girl. That thought troubled her, even confused her. In her mind, she knew that she was determined to work hard, but, was it destined for her to live as a servant of the Oliveira household? She wondered. She also entertained imaginary thoughts of how it could be like to be the daughter in law of a well-to-do Ferrao household, the opportunity she had left behind. A sudden shiver ran through her body, the evening breeze intensifying the chill, she tugged the ole tightly around her body as a stab of anxiety pierced her heart making it throb faster than usual, when she thought of the opportunity that could have possibly changed the financial and social status of her family.

With the Portuguese folks speaking among themselves, Claudia felt alone with nothing to do and no one really to talk to.

Her eyes were on Damiáno, who was sitting among the elders to discuss. She could see that he had respect among the top officials. They took his talk and advice seriously. White skinned girls hovered around him for attention. She was seeing a different side of Damiáno; a side where he came across as professional, extremely wise, strong, in command, and in demand. So it wasn't only her community that she had to be alert before being seen with him. His community would be equally let down, if they learnt about his relationship with Claudia, it would seem.

By afternoon, three local men had come with foodstuff for Tia Lourdes and her husband. Claudia was hungry, sleepy too after being awake through the night. She lay on the straw mat that Tia Lourdes had handed her to rest. In that corner of the kitchen, as she lay on the mat, she had a dream. In her dream Bula was fighting with the community elders. Then Bula picked up a big stone and hit one of them, that's when the elders, one by one, began to chase Bula until they caught her and tied her down with a rope. Claudia made moaning sounds in her sleep, but there was no one around to hear it. When she woke up and sat herself down, she wiped the spittle from her mouth. 'Was there trouble back home?' she wondered, based on the disturbing dream she just had.

The Portuguese folks were still in discussion. Indians and Portuguese. The military base. Portuguese and Indians. Advancing Indian forces. General Manuel António Vassalo e Silva. Jawaharlal Nehru. António de Oliveira Salazar. Structures demolished. The Portuguese soldiers. Continuous news buzzed in. Some bad, some normal, the worst rumour of it all was that Goa would be destroyed before being handed over to the Indians.

Later that afternoon, when the sun was changing its colour to a dullish amber and when Tia Lourdes' backyard seemed dead and motionless the three local men who claimed to have come to meet Tia Lourdes' husband made an exit. Perturbed by the dream she had, Claudia asked the men if they could give her a ride to Oroshim. They were kind to agree.

A new thought brought a sudden halt to every other thought running through her mind. She was still in Goa. She felt safe and secure. She could still turn and go back. And wouldn't the Portuguese return to Goa once the war was over? She remembered how much Paklin Bai loved Goa, so it was almost certain that once it gets peaceful again she would be back, which meant that Oliveira Bab would also be back and then obviously for more than one reason, Damiáno would also be back. She began to reason things out in her heart. Can she return back once she goes to Portugal? She wondered and then immediately negated the thought, realising that there was no way she could come back to Oroshim if she escaped to Portugal, especially not when the community gets to know the real reason for her escape.

Jakin's words began to repeat naggingly in her mind 'If coming back is the slightest option in your mind, please stop yourself right now. I plead with you.' Claudia knew that Jakin was right, but she had chosen to opt for the risk in the hope of pursuing a lifetime with Damiáno. At this moment, she wasn't sure of anything. Would her hope be fulfilled? She couldn't tell.

So far nothing was clear. One thing she knew, if she delayed staying out too long, even one night, she will lose the chance of being accepted back at Oroshim.

She took soft steps, doing her best not to make any noise as she peeped into one of the bedrooms where some of them including Paklin Bai were sleeping. Claudia quietly tiptoed towards the side of the bed where Paklin Bai was lying down. She called out to her softly after standing silently for a while, realising how tired Paklin Bai must be. She watched Paklin Bai sleep, observing the rhythmic rise and fall of her breathing and listening to her soft snores, and felt uncomfortable to disturb her sleep, not sure how she might react but she also didn't have the heart to sneak out of the house without telling anyone.

As for Damiáno, she was too scared to tell him that she wanted to return to Oroshim. Firstly, there was no privacy to talk to him alone and even if there was privacy, she could not get herself to look at him in the eye and tell him she wanted to go back home and not accompany him to Portugal.

'Claudia,' Paklin Bai suddenly rose up, startled to see Claudia standing near her bedside.

'Paklin Bai I am going.'

'Going? Going where?'

'To Oroshim. Mother will worry about me, I didn't tell her....'

'What? You didn't tell Busha? Damiáno said it's all taken care of. Damiáno!' She called out. Claudia shushed her, gesturing with her finger on her lips. 'Please don't call Damiáno Bab or anyone. I just want to go.'

For a moment Paklin Bai looked dumbstruck, her sleepy eyes widened, not expecting Claudia to have come away without informing her mother. Although Claudia and her mother worked for them as maids, Paklin Bai treated them both with much dignity and respect. She was a kind hearted woman, who appreciated things done in a proper manner. She quickly got out of bed, glancing around to make sure their talk wasn't being overheard, reached out and took Claudia's hand firmly and said 'Come' as she led her to the backyard where the boatmen were untying their canoes.

'They said they have space in their canoes.' Claudia reminded her as they moved briskly towards the shore.

'Yes, you are right Claudia, they have space,' Paklin Bai responded, looking at the canoes and finding them not occupied.

'Claudia, will you be fine with them?' she questioned, with a slightly worried expression.

'I will be Paklin Bai,' Claudia said softly with a tinge of uncertainty in her voice.

Gusts of breeze blew forcefully as the two women stood there for a moment. A draft of wind hit towards Paklin Bai, catching a few strands of her soft golden hair, partly covering her face. The large silky frill of her embroidered blouse flapped as she stood, looking elegant in her brightly coloured taffeta skirt, staring into Claudia's eyes, perturbed with what was happening. Claudia stood still, her eyes troubled, teary, looking small in comparison to Paklin Bai's tall European frame.

Both looked strangely into each other's eyes, then with a warm embrace, they both said goodbye to each other, both wanting to say something more, and wishing they didn't have to part this way. Claudia walked away swiftly, turning back several times watching Paklin Bai walk inside Tia Lourdes' house.

Claudia had got into the men's canoe, as if she was in a trance but she wasn't. She was very much in her senses. If she had the freedom to go by what her heart wanted, she wouldn't be anywhere else but where Damiáno was. Though, in her time alone at Tia Lourdes' place, it had dawned on her that tagging along with him was not just harmful for her but for him too. Every community, class and culture had its own tendencies to discriminate the other, she had learnt lately. Her senses had just opened up to that realisation, if his community had found out about what the two shared intimately, he could lose face with his kin, just like she would with hers. The dream about Bula fighting the community elders had seemed so real too, it was on her mind all the time. Every worrying thought seemed to have won in convincing her that she didn't fit under Tia Lourdes' roof.

In the canoe, the men kept their voices low as they discussed the events that followed through the day. Claudia strained her ears to hear, letting go only when it got audibly hard to listen to their chat. Where is the point anymore? In her mind Claudia questioned. None of the Portuguese folks had noticed her leave; neither Bab nor Damiáno. Only Paklin Bai.

Covered with her Mother's soft white ole, in silence, among the men in the canoe, Claudia got rowed to get to the other side. Is this the way it all had to finish? She turned back, still hoping Damiáno would notice that she had left and that someone would alert Damiáno about it. She had told Paklin Bai not to let Damiáno know about her leaving, yet she wished he came to know about it. Her own silliness embarrassed her. Water rippled roughly as the oars hit it hard. Yet again, she wondered if she should have stayed back at Tia Lourdes' villa, to travel to Portugal where she could spend the rest of her life being around the love of her life, Damiáno. Too late. The canoe men were afraid to be found getting food for the Portuguese, they wouldn't turn back even if she would plead. And now, suddenly she longed to see him, to search in his eyes, what it was that he had for her. Too late, she repeated in her mind. The decision was made, though she knew that no decision could ever seem right to kill an intimacy that was so overpowering. Her mind replayed many moments that she and Damiáno shared together; that authoritative voice that drew her to him. Their secret glances. All those crumpled paper balls of meet-me notes. The cycle rides to get away from Oroshim, their physical togetherness that seemed so right to her, each time. Anyone finding out about it would have called it sinful acts, breaking community rules. Let them, she thought. She rebelled in her mind.

She turned again but there was no one in the backyard, the Portuguese families too preoccupied with their own kith and kin, their own worries. The men in the canoe hurried to get across before dark; they said they had come with food as a sign of respect and faithfulness to their *Patrao*, the Portuguese term for boss. And now, so as not to be seen doing so, they rowed back speedily. The wind got colder, as the men got off the canoe to anchor it by the river bank. They hastened through the bushy bougainvilleas to untie their bicycles, secured with a rope to a coconut trunk. 'Oroshim is roughly an hour's distance by cycling but longer than that, by foot,' the men told Claudia.

Hitchhiking a ride on one of their bicycles, Claudia got to the main road. Thereafter, she walked alone, her hungry stomach making funny sounds inside her. She mumbled a prayer each time she sighted a soldier. Occasionally she slowed to ask the direction to Oroshim. Some men were heard discussing that the Indian armed forces had advanced towards Goa's capital, Panjim. The Portuguese has already surrendered, they spoke. Claudia did not bother to ask them any questions. She just wanted to get home before it got darker. Will the Oliveira family leave or will they stay back, now that they said the Portuguese have surrendered, Claudia wondered and wished for the latter. An hour of walking and she reached the cashew tree hills; the familiar place told her she wasn't too far from Oroshim as the chill got severe, the breeze crisper. After few more minutes of walking faster, she could see the pristine steeple standing alarmingly tall, as if it was reminding Claudia of the possible consequences. The church bell would ring any moment for Angelus. Claudia walked fast, halting suddenly at the Oroshim church gate. She wondered if she should go to Sankistao to find out if there was any tumult concerning her actions earlier in the morning. If Jakin told Mother, the news would first go to Gormai and the church authorities. Her fate and future would already have been pronounced, sealed by the elders. And that would be it. She hoped Jakin had kept things to herself, knowing well that she herself would not be the only victim of Jakin's truthfulness but Mother, Jakin and Bula; they all would suffer, if kicked out of the village.

December dew was falling freshly on the leaves and bushes, wetting them clean. Cold breeze from the fields nuzzled her tired body as she walked quietly through the empty bunds.

The evening fire burned under the water pot in her backyard. Jakin, obviously ignoring Claudia, was sitting in front of the fire, pushing dry leaves beneath the big copper pot; the evening routine of heating bath water. Claudia looked for Mother but Bula and Mother were not to be seen. In a way she was glad that Bula was out. The day had given her enough to take in Bula's sarcasm. 'The fool counts on the fish in the sea,' Bula had mocked her often with that proverb that the village folk used when one's expectation was higher than what they could achieve. She'd say it again, had she been there.

Shooing the little chicks out of her path, Claudia washed herself and stepped inside the house. Spreading a bamboo mat on the floor, she lay there tired, but thinking different things. Does the village know anything at all? If they do, it was already late. Oroshim was a place where gossip and rumours spread faster than fire over summer grass.

A little while later, Jakin stepped inside and began filling kerosene in the night lamp. 'Rice is warm. Go eat. Just the two of us for the night meal. Mother and Bula are out at the island feast. Mother had said they would be leaving after an early dinner, but you know the distance, it is more than two hours walk. Claudia, Mother was looking for you this morning; she assumed you went to the fields with Gormai. I didn't know how to tell her about you, so I didn't. Just when I was preparing to tell her all about it when she returns, you came back.' Jakin lit the lamp and continued, 'You're a wise girl Claudia. I know you came back for Mother. It would be hard to face the village if you didn't come back. All day, I had been thinking of ways to break the sad news of you leaving. Different versions, but none seemed right. Thank heavens you are back,' Jakin sounded like she was going to cry. 'Go eat, the weather is bad, food gets cold in no time. Should I serve and get it for you? Claudia!'

Jakin didn't get an answer; instead she heard a soft snoring. Jakin grinned to herself, wondering if her prodigal sister had even heard what she just said. Heading to the kitchen, Jakin began to pour kerosene in the kitchen lamp.

The war is over

The news was official. The Portuguese were leaving and Goa was not under Portuguese colonial rule anymore. The escudo would suddenly lose its valour in the Goan soils, making way for the Indian rupee. The repercussion of the sudden change, within a short time, would not be small; change in leadership, change in authority, change in the country, in the currency, it was a lot of change and would take time to sink into the local folk. 19 December, 1961 became the day the colonial rule of hundreds of years came to an end. Goa was now a part of India. The Portuguese Governor General Manuel António Vassalo e Silva signed the official document following the surrender.

Some Goans chose to leave with the Portuguese. Of course, many like Claudia, in spite of a close association with them, for various reasons, were still left behind. Estado da India, Portuguese India that is, no doubt, left an inerasable influence; their culture, their cuisine, their mannerisms, all of which would take a lifetime to forget, for some at least. 'The war is over,' naked-chested village kids, wearing only their house pants, were heard shouting out the slogan while hand pushing discarded cycle tyres as their toy vehicles.

New Year followed Christmas. The year 1962 replaced the much eventful 1961. Shortly, some of the Portuguese people, who were left behind during the time of liberation were transported to Portugal via Bombay. Political power and system in Goa changed completely along with the change in the season. With the winter subsiding, the wind in the meadow got warmer, causing a scarce fall of pre-summer leaves. The warm weather had wiped out the dewy dampness and the wintry glisten over trees, bushes and hilltop grass; a dry and earthy look all across. On the political front, the prisoners-of-war were sent off to Lisbon via Karachi, Pakistan.

Meanwhile, a new coat of white paint had replaced the green mold patches on church walls. As in every summer, the mud hut owners had begun to cover their homes with freshly thatched palms, while those owning country tiled roof homes had a realignment check done on roofs. Salt vendors, seated in bullock carts were heard shouting out to potential buyers. Overlooking the rising summer heat, folks in the fields continued their labour of long hours; drying and storing a sufficient harvest. Haystacks were restored, rice barns were filled to a brim, kitchen essentials like spice, onions, salted fish, pickled mangoes and wood for fire was stored to last the coming monsoon. Through all the routines of the season, the inhabitants of Oroshim warmed up to abundant sunshine, looking forward to Claudia's May wedding.

The sun was still up and the reapers still at the fields, when Bula initiated a happy dance right at the backyard, going about with the old style of the womenfolk; *Hath. Paim. Bonk.* They giggled silly as they did their moves without a care; first Bula, then Claudia. Jakin joined in, eventually dragging Mother to do it too. The silliness of the dance would embarrass them otherwise, but not today, not when there was a wedding going to take place at home, for the first time ever.

Passersby stopped to stare, grinning wide in amusement; anybody watching them would. Gormai's overwhelming smile showed that she wanted to dance too but nobody asked her to join, it was the dance of her times; a few silly ancient moves. Gormai hugged Claudia's Mother; something she had not done for years. The desperation for a wedding in the home was so strong that when it was happening at last, it had to change so many things; first of all, it ended the mother-in-law-daughter-in-law strife of years. 'Look up to the heavens and give thanks.' Gormai told Mother. The girls continued their dance. *Hath-Paim-Bonk.* Hands. Feet. Bum. Hands tapping hands. Palms tapping knees. Bums rubbing bums. Hands. Feet. Bum! *Hath. Paim. Bonk.*

The villagers, mostly generous during weddings in the locality, contributed their gifts and labour towards Claudia's wedding, working for days in preparation along with the wedding family. Men worked hard to do up the frontyard; the final outcome of which was the colourful streamers decorated mud walls as well as a wedding venue of palm bordered fencing with thick cloth canopies in the frontyard. They hung hired conical loudspeakers with ropes along tall coconut trees; the loudspeakers amplifying music and cheer across the usually quiet village of Oroshim.

That morning, the neighbourhood waited eagerly to see the bridegroom's people arriving at the bride's house; the customary calcada, expected any moment. As per tradition, they would bring along with them the bridal dress, the bride's bouquet, the bolce, the cushions, the bridesmaids' dresses, a new comb, powder for the bride's face, even a scent bottle and a few other things required to get the bride ready for the day.

After a warm water bath, Claudia sat under the backyard sun to dry her thick soap-nut rinsed hair; her eyes fixed towards the bund road, to check if the calcada was nearing home. One custom that Claudia never agreed on was the bride's crying. How could they expect a bride to cry on a happy day such as her wedding day? She had argued about it in the past. Not anymore, she had made up her mind to be discreet, deciding not to argue or highlight faults in the village system, now that she had found her own guide of survival. Probably, village folks expected the bride to show others that she was sad to leave her mother's house. That's why, if any bride failed to cry, she was likely to face the snare of village gossip. Many even put on an act of crying, just to please the community.

At the moment, Claudia's throat ached to cry out aloud, though it had nothing to do with the village tradition or leaving her mother's home. She had other things to deal with, the cause of heartache.

'I don't care who thinks I disqualify to be a bridesmaid, now that he confirmed it with the priests and with Gormai, I will proudly be that bridesmaid that Oroshim has never seen before. Watch me make them go green with envy. The best bridesmaid ever! He could choose anyone but he thought I would make the best bridesmaid.' Bula was all over the place, bragging about herself, and about what a great bridesmaid she would make, a look of unstoppable excitement clear in her face.

'He is a good man,' Claudia said, looking at Bula.

'Stop it now, enough showing off.'

'You stop Bula. I agree with Claudia. He is indeed a good man,' Jakin interrupted.

'Of course! Bride's big sister, of course, he is a good man! The good man better make sure that my nosy Gormai or any elder doesn't harass this bridesmaid, that's all. Claudia, you are sure he spoke to them about me, you're not lying to me, are you?'

'How many times will you ask the same question Bula? Yes. He told me himself.'

'I want to be sure no one troubles me. I hate those community elders, I hate Gormai. And the priests....'

'Ssshhh.'

'Don't ssshhh me you both. Claudia, when did he tell you that he spoke to them ... this same bridesmaid thing?'

'Yesterday.'

'You met him yesterday? Phew. Check it out folks; our bride just broke a custom.'

'Keep your voice low, Bula. I was not supposed to meet him. He was waiting for me at the Tanno, when Sankistao took me to buy handkerchiefs and slippers, I had no idea that it was he who told Sankistao to bring me along; he desired to look at my face, that's what he told Sankistao. I was not even supposed to tell you both that I met him. Now please,' Claudia's eyes glistened slightly, as she revealed it to her sisters.

‘I told you, this is getting more romantic than we want it to be. Lucky you! I have nothing much to say,’ Bula said. Twitching her nose and making silly faces, she walked away.

‘Bula is silly. Don’t mind her; everyone is happy for you. You better be good to him. He is a good man and has been kind to our family, especially the last few days. He didn’t ask for any dowry, you know well what that means to us, Claudia. Don’t ever let him down for anything,’ Jakin said in her preachy, older sister tone and began to comb Claudia’s hair. Claudia stayed silent. Strong odour of summer fruits wafted in; jackfruit cut open in backyards and barns, mangoes eaten plentifully, their leftover seeds thrown to crows to chew on. It was an air of mix fruit smell.

Sankistao walked in, limping his way to the girls. ‘Sankistao, we were just talking about you. You are going to live a hundred years,’ Claudia greeted him, quoting the customary proverb of the village, where they believed, if a person being discussed appeared, the person would live a hundred years.

‘Already limping at sixty-five, you girls want me to limp up to a hundred? The Almighty has not given that in any man’s hands, my dear. So! Is our bride ready?’

‘The bride is almost ready, Sankistao,’ Jakin answered softly.

‘Of course she will be. Can she go wrong with such a dear elder sister to help?’ Sankistao’s deliberate compliment left Jakin grinning proudly.

Elderly folk, with their rosary beads, waited inside the house to bless the bride. Most neighbours waited anxiously to see Claudia. Summer heat being at its peak, kids waited to drink the tangerine hued lemonade to be served at the wedding. Young men waited to woo young ladies on the dance floor. Many others waited for the delicious wedding menu; croquettes, green chutney sandwich, forminha, stew and sausage Pulao topped with a peas-potato-carrot mix. Men waited for beer, some womenfolk too, but secretly, since the chilled beverage was served only in the men's row.

As for Claudia, she didn't particularly look forward to anything. 'Shouldn't a bride feel elated on her wedding day? I somehow can't get that feeling, maybe I am not really ready for this.'

'Did someone say anything to you, Claudia?' Sankistao questioned, taken aback by her unexpected words.

'No. But I feel as if ...'

'As if?'

'As if, something is left behind and as if someone is yet to show up here to see me. Damiáno Bab ...'

'Enough of that, girl, we are no more a part of Portuguese India. I know our men sitting in taverns continue to complain about how they miss the Portuguese queijo and their olive oil coated Bacalhau, and our old women still talk about how charming and generous those white men were with them. As for the keepers of the essentials shops, they do grumble how costly the onions and oil have soared up, after the Portuguese have left. Nevertheless, and whether we like it or not, the Portuguese are never coming back to be with us. We are a part of India now. It's time we settled that in our minds, and it's time you stopped waiting for Damiáno Bab. He is not coming back, Claudia.'

'Well, maybe he is not. I still can't deny him completely, can I? I must confess it all to Padkur; tell Gormai and the elders about it. And Piedade, shouldn't he know that my heart belongs to Damiáno Bab alone? I must tell him, Sankistao. Mustn't I?' As Claudia opened up, her mouth shivered to cry.

Exchanging a worried look, Jakin and Sankistao helplessly watched Claudia weaken herself with her emotions about a past that no one could do anything about, and Sankistao with his age and experience could empathise with her. Inching closer, he tried to calm the bride-to-be, his words coming almost in whispers. 'Listen to me; you are becoming a wife today. Soon, you will learn real matters about life. You will learn that people make mistakes. And none is perfect. The ones who claim to be, often pretend to be perfect, but they are not. It is true that people come into our lives, but not all of them will stay with us, dear. Hear it from me, sometimes the ones very dearest to our heart will leave us and go, and that must hurt, I know it. But it doesn't mean we give up on life, because of those sad feelings.'

'It wasn't a feeling Sankistao, and definitely not a sad one. It was real, he made me happy and I doubt if anyone can make me happy, like Bab did. Tell me, what then? It wasn't a feeling but truthfulness about ...'

'Kill that truthfulness,' Jakin snapped angrily, her voice overpowering, and though the brashness of her words stunned Sankistao, his heart went out to Claudia, for her naive honesty, compelling him even more to find a way to convince her to take a wise decision. 'Go girl; hear it from your big sister. She has a bad experience behind her,' he said.

It was Sankistao who had volunteered to support the girls, especially Claudia, after they had lost their father, and it certainly would be disheartening to see Claudia back out of the marriage at that last hour. Not when she had come so close to making it happen for herself and her family.

'How does one kill truth?' Claudia questioned, narrowing her eyes, her voice choking and tears running down her face.

'Claudia, this is the life that your parents and our community elders had always dreamed for you. What you have before you right now is many Oroshim girls' dream. Can you even afford to play with it, girl? Let me tell you something my dear, when we go looking for a match for our village girls, we long to find a well settled man like Piedade, we rarely do. Sadly. But, we did find someone like him for you. Won't you let us celebrate it with you? Is it fair that all you feel is someone missing?' Sankistao spoke as calmly as he could. 'The elders can be ruthless and punishing. If you can trust me enough, I'd like to say that one should never let them discover anyone's wrongs. Hear it from me dear, as good as they are to you now, they won't think twice if they have to stop you from entering the church or working at the fields. Think of your mother and sisters, didn't they have their share of punishment? You must help them, Claudia, and I know you will. Be wise, is all I want to say.' After stopping to talk for a moment, Sankistao drew in a deep breath and said, 'Look up to the heavens. There is only one who can judge us of our wrongs. Let me remind you girl, I have lived in this village long enough to know that there is no mercy for wrongdoers here. I am not misleading you to tell them lies, but you cannot tell it all to them. You three are like daughters to me. Pardon this old man if he has said something more than what he should have; however, the choice is still yours.'

Claudia didn't need any convincing that Sankistao cared and that he said those things out of concern, she even agreed in her mind that she should be concealing some things and decide the best way out, yet, she couldn't help her feelings. She felt just like the way she did when she walked away from Tia Lourdes' house. 'No decision could be termed right in such a situation,' she had told herself, unable to name her decision wrong or right, when she had decided to walk away from Damiáno and his family. It wasn't only the dream about Bula fighting the elders that had made her come back home nor the worry that her family would be cast out of the village, not even the thought of compromising to live as a housemaid all her life; though it was all of it but there was still more reason for her to walk away, the way she did.

It was Damiáno, she loved him very much, even unto death, her heart well convinced of it. However, on spur of that moment, perchance by her own speculation, she had felt like a gruelling, stumbling block to his reputation and sadly, he to hers. Most in the village told her that this was it that she would have to do, though much before they could tell her, she had brought herself to a logical verdict, whereby she knew she had to say yes to a solemn marriage with Piedade Ferrao.

Gormai's loud voice jarred the backyard where Jakin, Claudia and Sankistao stood discussing. 'Are you here to hurry the bride or delay her?' Gormai asked, hinting sarcastically at Sankistao.

'Just a last minute advice, Adelina.'

'Can anything anger a man more than somebody holding back the sight of his lady love from him? Do I have to tell you, Abel? You should know.'

'I do know Adelina. Go girl; get your bridegroom before it gets late and before your grandmother starts a war with me.' Sankistao said chuckling, looking Claudia in the eye, the look in his eyes assuring her not to worry, that it would all be fine in the end.

'None of us can offer the girl a better advice than what life itself will reveal,' Gormai mumbled through her friendly banter with Sankistao. She hurried Claudia to put on her bridal clothes, now that the calcada had arrived. Claudia washed her face of all the saltiness of tears, Jakin following her quickly with a towel in hand. 'Don't cry anymore, Claudia. Piedade will take good care of you. Sankistao is right. Be wise before you reveal anything to the elders. And if Damiáno Bab and his memories are really special, they don't deserve to go out in public, don't you think so? Keep them closed in the special place of your heart as Saudade.'

'Saudade?'

'Yes. It is a longing of the heart. Selfless, harmless love that stays on in your being, as a strong memory, the way it was, when it was. Saudade!'

'Saudade!' Claudia repeated softly after Jakin, realising now, that saudade it was that had kept Jakin emotionally going. Jakin smiled at that assurance of being understood. At that moment, it wasn't any audible moans or hugs that helped the sisters express the love they had for one another, one thing that they had always found hard to express, in the family. All that was bottled inside of them was now coming out through those moments of bonding and confessing.

'You mean live life on memories? I don't think I am as humble as you Jakin. Though saudade has its own beauty, and I like it much, it suits you more. As for me, I doubt I can dwell in two places; either I sit back in my past stubbornly and never move forward, or, if I do move, I walk forward and never look back. It's a hard decision, but I'll do it. So tell me now, what do I do? What would you do if you were in my place, Jakin?' Claudia wept again. Jakin wept too, leaving the question unanswered.

In the sitting room, the elders began to bless the bride customarily. Ready in her white bridal attire, Claudia sat, tears still forming in her eyes. It was Jakin's turn to bless, she hugged her and whispered, 'Now that you look so beautiful in these white clothes, don't look back. Just move forward,' Jakin advised. Most elders gathered at home, advised and blessed the bride circling around as she left home to get to the church for the wedding nuptials.

When all the wedding customs were done with, Claudia settled into her husband's home. The summer heat began to simmer down with the first rains in early June. The same month, the first Lieutenant Governor of Goa, Daman and Diu took his official position. The change flowed along. Goa was to get accustomed to the new political system and more. Claudia, on the other hand, was to accustom herself to a change of a different sort. She had lived in lack most of her days in her mother's mud house, and now, she was to live in Piedade's abundant home, watching servants cook sumptuous food and serve at the table every day. She was to eat the plenty of her husband's home; the place where it wouldn't take her any toiling to make ends meet, where there will be no sisterly strife or pillow fights, nor an escaping in the dark hours to be tempted for a man's carnal touch.

Shortly, Claudia learned to oversee the cash flow coming from the sale of coconuts, the paddy, the dairy and other produce of her father-in-law's fields and land. She did well with helping out in the affairs of the Ferrao household, while Piedade, her husband, resumed his job on the ship after a long wedding break.

On most nights, Claudia slept well with the comfort of a soft pillow and clean sheets in their high roofed bedroom. Occasionally, on a rainy morning, she sat down to write a letter to her husband. Rubbing her palm fondly over her protruding four-month belly, she stood, often, by a window that overlooked the vast stretches of paddy fields and land, coconuts from tall palms, the riches that came from their backyard farm, the milk, the dung cakes drying on coconut trunks, freshly laid chicken eggs, pigs being slaughtered regularly; all of it sold in the market for good money. The Ferraos had garnered much wealth, which the child in Claudia's womb was going to inherit. The kind of wealth that makes you feel mystical about, the kind of wealth that makes you feel you were alone through a journey, and you alone know where you've been and the risks you took, to call that wealth yours. It was how Claudia felt, at times.

Some of Claudia's days in her husband's absence were lazy, some were nauseating, with her fast progressing pregnancy. Some days it rained heavily. Some days were nasty to bring back memories of a concealed past. With elderly in-laws in the house; respected much in the community, she had to be careful not to give her past any audacity to surface. Her husband Piedade, older to her by more than ten years, was well known among the elders of the land. Being the only daughter-in-law, she was expected to guard the reputation of the Ferrao household. Sometimes, there would be a visit from Bula, Jakin or Mother. At times Gormai would come and spend a day with Claudia and her in-laws. Sankistao and Padkur would visit her too.

Anybody meeting Claudia post marriage could see a change in her; the facial features and her behaviour brought out a sudden maturity. The look on her face was more serious and her talk more focused, in comparison to the earlier child-like laughter and mannerisms. Earlier, she had a bold readiness to argue over things unjust, when she had a sweet innocence and a certain gullibility which matched that innocence. In the past, she had twinkles that rimmed her eyes as she smiled. It was all gone. She had traded it all for a life of survival, it seemed.

The community folk and elders were pleased with Claudia.

Acknowledgements

'Claudia' was made possible with unstinted support of a few special individuals whose contribution I would like to acknowledge:

The awesome leaders and everyone who worked with exceptional efficiency behind the scenes from my Publisher, Niyogi Books.

Suhail Mathur, my brilliant literary agent from The Book Bakers.

My parents Sylvester Lorena and Claudina Mergulhao, who taught me to face life with boldness and cheer, in spite of everything.

My brothers and sisters, Maria, Bento, Karmen, Roshan and their families for all the times of togetherness and laughter.

My children and greatest motivation, Sean and Shamyra.

And above all, Jesus, for the Love, Wisdom and Ideas to write this book.